Eileen Colwell

After gaining her Diploma of Librarianship
at University College, London, Eileen Colwell
spent two years at Bolton Library before moving
to Hendon in North London in 1926. There
was no library service for children there at that
time, so she started one. During her time as
Borough Children's Librarian, Hendon Children's Library became famous in many parts of
the world, a tribute to a pioneer in the field of
children's reading. When the new Borough of
Barnet was formed, Miss Colwell continued
as Librarian in charge of work with children,
with an even larger number of schools and
libraries under her care.

Eileen Colwell was Chairman for five years
of the International Federation of Library
Associations' committee on library work with
children, and she was a member of the Carnegie
Medal Committee of the Library Association
from its first award in 1936 until shortly before
her retirement.

Storytelling has always been her special
interest and joy, and it has taken her to many
parts of Britain, to Holland, the United States
and Canada and Japan. In the 1965 New Year
Honours she was awarded the MBE for her
unique services to children's libraries and books.
Now retired from her lectureship at the Lough-
borough School of Librarianship, she still
tours the country, continuing the storytelling
that has always been her special interest. In
1974 she was made an honorary Fellow of
Manchester Polytechnic, and in 1975 Lough-
borough University awarded her the honorary
degree of Doctor of Letters.

HUMBLEPUPPY
AND OTHER STORIES
FOR TELLING

Words

Out of us all
That make rhymes,
Will you choose
Sometimes—
As the winds use
A crack in a wall
Or a drain,
Their joy or their pain
To whistle through—
Choose me,
You English words?

From *Collected Poems*
by Edward Thomas
(Faber & Faber)

HUMBLEPUPPY
AND OTHER
STORIES
FOR TELLING

With notes on how
to tell them by
EILEEN COLWELL
Drawings by
RON MARIS

THE BODLEY HEAD
LONDON SYDNEY
TORONTO

British Library Cataloguing
in Publication Data
Humblepuppy and other stories for telling.
1.   Children's stories
1.   Colwell, Eileen
823'.9'1J   PZ5
ISBN 0–370–30127–7

Printed and bound in Great Britain for
The Bodley Head Ltd
9 Bow Street, London WC2E 7AL
by BAS Printers Limited, Over Wallop, Hampshire
set in Monophoto Apollo
First published 1978

Acknowledgments

Every effort has been made to trace the ownership of the copyright
material in this book. It is the publishers' belief that the necessary
permissions from publishers, authors, and authorised agents have been
obtained, but in the event of any question arising as to the use of any
material, the publishers, while expressing regret for any error
unconsciously made, will be pleased to make the necessary corrections
in future editions of this book.

Thanks are due to the following for permission to reprint copyright
material: Miss Myfanwy Thomas for 'Words' from *Collected Poems by
Edward Thomas*, published by Faber & Faber Ltd; Joan Aiken
Enterprises Ltd for 'Humblepuppy' from *A Harp of Fishbones*, published
by Jonathan Cape Ltd; Miss Anne Wolfe as the literary executor of the
late Humbert Wolfe for 'The House of Ghosts' from *Twentieth Century
Poetry* edited by Harold Munro, published by Chatto & Windus; Mr E.
R. Eratne for 'How the Lizard Fought the Leopard' from *Folk Tales from
Asia. Vol. 2*, edited by Eileen Colwell and Kyoko Matsuoka, published
under the Asian Copublication Programme; William Heinemann Ltd for
'Peter's Mermaid' from *Charlotte Hough's Holiday Book* by Charlotte
Hough; Hutchinson Publishing Group Ltd for 'Prot and Krot' from *The
Amber Mountain and other folk stories*, by Agnes Szudek, published by
Hutchinson Junior Books; The Literary Trustees of Walter de la Mare
and The Society of Authors as their representative for 'The Dutch
Cheese' from *Collected Stories for Children* by Walter de la Mare,
published by Faber & Faber Ltd; George G. Harrap & Company Ltd and
The Viking Press for 'The Little Brown Bees of Ballyvourney' from *Told
on the King's Highway* by Eleanore Myers Jewett, Copyright 1943 by
Eleanore Myers Jewett, renewed © 1971 by C. Harvey Jewett;
Macmillan, London and Basingstoke, for 'Flannan Isle' from *Collected
Poems* by Wilfrid Gibson; Routledge & Kegan Paul Ltd for 'The Little
Wee Tyke' from *Forgotten Folktales of the English Counties*, collected by
Ruth Tongue; Associated Book Publishers Ltd for 'The Dog' from *The
Adventures of Mandy Duck* by Donald Bisset, published by Methuen
Children's Books Ltd; David Higham Associates for 'Golden Hair' and 'A
Box on the Ear' from *A Book of Ghosts and Goblins* by Ruth Manning-
Sanders, published by Methuen Children's Books Ltd; 'Little Holger and
his Flute' from Johan Fabricius: *The Devil in the Tower: Seven Diabolical*

Tales, translated by Lance Salway (Longman Young Books, 1973) pp. 33–46. Copyright © 1971 by Johan Fabricius. English translation copyright © 1973 by Longman Young Books, reprinted by permission of Penguin Books Ltd; MacGibbon & Kee Ltd/Granada Publishing Ltd and Harcourt Brace Jovanovich, Inc. for 'hist, whist' from *The Complete Poems of e. e. cummings 1913–1962*, Copyright, 1923, renewed 1951 by e. e. cummings; William Collins Sons & Co Ltd for 'The Duchess of Houndsditch' from *West of Widdershins* by Barbara Sleigh; Victor Gollancz Ltd and Doubleday & Co. Inc. for 'The Princess and the Pea' from *Hans Andersen: His Classic Fairytales*, translated by Erik Haugaard; The Estate of the late Ogden Nash and Little Brown & Co. for 'The Adventures of Isabel' from *Many Long Years Ago* by Ogden Nash, published by J. M. Dent; A. D. Peters & Co Ltd for 'The Fog Horn' from *The Golden Apples of the Sun* by Ray Bradbury, published by Hart-Davis MacGibbon Ltd; The Bodley Head Ltd and The Viking Press for 'Schnitzle, Schnotzle and Schnootzle' from *The Long Christmas* by Ruth Sawyer, Copyright 1941, © 1969 by Ruth Sawyer; Hamish Hamilton Children's Books Ltd for 'Baba Yaga and the Little Girl with the Kind Heart' from *Old Peter's Russian Tales* by Arthur Ransome; David Higham Associates Limited for 'The Rainbow' from *A Walk to the Hills of the Dreamtime* by James Vance Marshall, published by Hodder & Stoughton; Iwanami Shoten, Publishers, for 'The Magic Drum' by Momoko Ishii, translated by Kyoko Matsuoka and adapted by Eileen Colwell; Harcourt Brace Jovanovich, Inc. for 'What did you put in your Pocket?' from *Something Special* by Beatrice Schenk de Regniers, © 1958 by Beatrice Schenk de Regniers; Harper & Row, Publishers, Inc. for 'A Christmas Story' from 'The Trapper's Tale of the First Birthday' from *This Way to Christmas* by Ruth Sawyer. Copyright, 1916, 1924, by Harper & Row, Publishers, Incorporated. Copyright, 1944, by Ruth Sawyer Durand. Copyright, 1952, by Maginel Wright Barney.

Contents

The Hopping Halfpenny

Every day Paddy left his cottage, walked along the road past the baker's shop and the post office, over the bridge and along the lane to the stile. There he stopped and lighted his pipe.

One day as he leant on the stile, thinking of nothing at all, he heard a sound at his feet—*tap, tap, chink, chink*. A tiny halfpenny was hopping up and down, up and down, all by itself in the sunshine, as if it were alive.

'That's queer!' thought Paddy. 'I wonder could I catch it, mebbe, and take it home?'

He stooped and put his right hand under it. *Plop!* It fell softly into his palm and he slipped his left hand over it to keep it safe. Then he set out for home, the halfpenny hopping gently between his two hands.

Along the lane, across the bridge, past the post office and the baker's shop went Paddy and turned into his own door.

'Biddy! Biddy!' he shouted. 'Will you be looking at what I've found.'

'I will not,' said his wife. 'I'm making the stirabout for dinner.'

'Come now—it's a living wonder I'll be showing you,' pleaded Paddy.

9

His wife came from the kitchen wiping her hands on her apron. Paddy opened his hands and the halfpenny hopped out and bounced up and down on the well-scrubbed table.

'It's alive!' exclaimed Biddy. 'I never saw the like! I must fetch Widow Maloney to see it.'

In came Widow Maloney with her boy Patrick.

In came Mrs O'Shea with her girl Nora.

In came Granny McConachie with her cat.

In came Michael Moriarty with his fiddle tucked under his arm. Everyone stared at the hopping halfpenny, their eyes popping out of their heads with astonishment.

'Bedad!' said Widow Maloney. 'You must take the wee thing to the Fair, Paddy. It's a fortune you could make with a wonder like that.'

'You'd be able to leave this old place,' said Mrs O'Shea.

'No more stirabout for you,' said Granny McConachie.

'I'll not be taking it to the Fair,' said Paddy. 'The wee thing mightn't be liking it.'

Michael Moriarty began to play a lively tune on his fiddle. The children danced round the room and the halfpenny hopped in time to the music. More and more people came in and by tea-time every person in the village had seen the wonderful hopping halfpenny.

'Be off with you all,' said Biddy at last. 'Leave us be till tomorrow.' So everyone went home but the halfpenny went on hopping just the same.

That evening Paddy and Biddy sat on their creepie stools on either side of the glowing peat fire. On the warm hearth the halfpenny hopped quietly, the old black cat watching it as if it were a mouse.

'Sure and all,' said Paddy, 'it's like having the children back again. The wee thing is company, so it is. But what shall we do to keep it safe tonight? I'd not like it to be stolen or hopping away when me back's turned.'

At last they decided to shut it up in Paddy's tobacco tin. Then they went to bed.

They had scarcely fallen asleep when they were wakened by a noise downstairs. *Thump, thump!*

'Lord save us!' whispered Biddy. 'A thief! Go down and catch him, man.'

'Not me!' said Paddy, putting his head under the bedclothes.

Thump, thump, thump, thump! The banging and clattering were enough to wake the Seven Sleepers.

'Will ye listen now!' said Biddy. 'Mebbe he's stealing the best teapot . . . Find out what that noise is, or I'll set about you!'

She pushed Paddy out of bed and he stood shivering at the top of the steep staircase, the candle in his hand. The noise in the kitchen below was deafening. The house shook with the *thump, thump.*

Slowly and unwillingly Paddy went halfway down the stairs—caught his foot and fell down the rest of the way and rolled into the kitchen.

The tobacco tin was bouncing up and down the table as if it were alive. It hit the ceiling with a thump that brought the plaster down and jarred Paddy from head to foot.

Suddenly he realised what was happening. 'Sure, it's the hopping halfpenny!' he exclaimed with relief. He saw his chance, clapped his hand on the tin as it struck the table and held on to it for dear life. He opened the tin and the hopping halfpenny shot up to the ceiling again. As it fell, Paddy caught it in his hand.

'Whisha, whisha!' he said softly. 'Gently now. There's no call to make such a strotheration. I'll not keep you if it's not to your liking. Am I to take you back to where I found you?'

At once the hopping halfpenny stopped its frantic bouncing and hopped up and down gently.

Paddy put his right hand under the halfpenny and closed his left hand over it to keep it safe. Then, just as he was, in his nightshirt, he stepped out into the empty street. The moon was shining and everything was very still. Down the road he walked, past the baker's shop and the post office, across the bridge and along the road to the stile.

There he knelt down and opened his hand and the hopping

halfpenny plopped on to the stone. For a moment it hopped gaily up and down, up and down, in the moonlight, then it gave a great leap right out of sight.

And although Paddy came to the stile many times to look for the hopping halfpenny, he never saw it again.

Traditional. Adapted by Eileen Colwell
(See Note, page 154)

The House of Ghosts

First to describe the house. Who has not seen it
  once at the end of an evening's walk—the leaves
that suddenly open, and as sudden screen it
  with the first flickering hint of shadowy eaves?

Was there a light in the high window? Or
  only the moon's cool candle palely lit?
Was there a pathway leading to the door?
  Or only grass and none to walk on it?

And surely someone cried, 'Who goes there—who?'
  And ere the lips could shape the whispered 'I,'
the same voice rose, and chuckled, 'You, 'tis you!'
  A voice, or the furred night-owl's human cry?

Who has not seen the house? Who has not started
  towards the gate half-seen, and paused, half-fearing,
and half beyond all fear—and the leaves parted
  again, and there was nothing in the clearing?

Humbert Wolfe
From *Twentieth Century Poetry*
edited by Harold Munro
(Chatto & Windus)

Humblepuppy

Our house was furnished mainly from auction sales. When you buy furniture that way you get a lot of extra things besides the particular piece that you were after, since the stuff is sold in lots: Lot 13, two Persian rugs, a set of golf-clubs, a sewing-machine, a walnut radio-cabinet, and a plinth.

It was in this way that I acquired a tin deedbox, which came with two coal-scuttles and a broom cupboard. The deedbox is solid metal, painted black, big as a medium-sized suitcase. When I first brought it home I put it in my study, planning to use it as a kind of filing-cabinet for old typescripts. I had gone into the kitchen, and was busy arranging the brooms in their new home, when I heard a loud thumping coming from the direction of the study.

I went back, thinking that a bird must have flown through the window; no bird, but the banging seemed to be inside the deedbox. I had already opened it as soon as it was in my possession, to see if there were any diamonds or bearer bonds worth thousands of pounds inside (there weren't), but I opened it again. The key was attached to the handle by a thin chain. There was nothing inside. I shut it. The banging started again. I opened it.

14

Still nothing inside.

Well, this was broad daylight, two o'clock on Thursday afternoon, people going past in the road outside and a radio schools programme chatting away to itself in the next room. It was not a ghostly kind of time, so I put my hand into the empty box and moved it about.

Something shrank away from my hand. I heard a faint, scared whimper. It could almost have been my own, but wasn't. Knowing that someone—something?—else was afraid too put heart into me. Exploring carefully and gently around the interior of the box I felt the contour of a small, bony, warm, trembling body with big awkward feet, and silky dangling ears, and a cold nose that, when I found it, nudged for a moment anxiously but trustingly into the palm of my hand. So I knelt down, put the other hand into the box as well, cupped them under a thin little ribby chest, and lifted out Humblepuppy.

He was quite light.

I couldn't see him, but I could hear his faint inquiring whimper, and I could hear his toenails scratch on the floorboards.

Just at that moment the cat, Taffy, came in.

Taffy has a lot of character. Every cat has a lot of character, but Taffy has more than most, all of it inconvenient. For instance, although he is sociable, and longs for company, he just despises company in the form of dogs. The mere sound of a dog barking two streets away is enough to make his fur stand up like a porcupine's quills and his tail swell like a mushroom cloud.

Which it did the instant he saw Humblepuppy.

Now here is the interesting thing. I could hear and feel Humblepuppy, but couldn't see him; Taffy, apparently, could see and smell him, but couldn't feel him. We soon discovered this. For Taffy, sinking into a low, gladiator's crouch, letting out all the time a fearsome throaty wauling like a bagpipe revving up its drone, inched his way along to where Humblepuppy huddled trembling by my left foot, and then dealt him what ought to have been a swinging right-handed clip on the ear. 'Get out of my house, you filthy little canine scum!' was what he was plainly intending to convey.

15

But the swipe failed to connect; instead it landed on my shin. I've never seen a cat so astonished. It was like watching a kitten meet itself for the first time in a looking-glass. Taffy ran round to the back of where Humblepuppy was sitting: felt; smelt; poked gingerly with a paw; leapt back nervously; crept forward again. All the time Humblepuppy just sat, trembling a little, giving out this faint beseeching sound that meant: 'I'm only a poor little mongrel without a smidgeon of harm in me. *Please* don't do anything nasty! I don't even know how I came here.'

It certainly was a puzzle how he had come. I rang the auctioneers (after shutting Taffy *out* and Humblepuppy *in* to the study with a bowl of water and a handful of Boniebisk, Taffy's favourite breakfast food).

The auctioneers told me that Lot 12, deedbox, coal-scuttles and broom cupboard, had come from Riverland Rectory, where Mr Smythe, the old rector, had lately died aged ninety. Had he ever possessed a dog, or a puppy? They couldn't say; they had merely received instructions from a firm of lawyers to sell the furniture.

I never did discover how poor little Humblepuppy's ghost got into that deedbox. Maybe he was shut in by mistake, long ago, and suffocated; maybe some callous Victorian gardener dropped him, box and all, into a river, and the box was later found and fished out.

Anyway, and whatever had happened in the past, now that Humblepuppy had come out of his box, he was very pleased with the turn his affairs had taken, ready to be grateful and affectionate. As I sat typing I'd often hear a patter-patter, and feel his small chin fit itself comfortably over my foot, ears dangling. Goodness knows what kind of a mixture he was; something between a terrier and a spaniel, I'd guess. In the evening, watching television or sitting by the fire, one would suddenly feel his warm weight leaning against one's leg. (He didn't put on a lot of weight while he was with us, but his bony little ribs filled out a bit.)

For the first few weeks we had a lot of trouble with Taffy, who was very surly over the whole business and blamed me bitterly for not getting rid of this low-class intruder. But Humblepuppy was extremely placating, got back into his deedbox whenever the atmosphere became too volcanic, and did his very best not to be a nuisance.

By and by Taffy thawed. As I've said he is really a very sociable cat. Although quite old, seventy cat years, he dearly likes cheerful company, and generally has some young cat friend who comes to play with him, either in the house or the garden. In the last few years we've had Whisky, the black-and-white pub cat, who used to sit washing the smell of fish-and-chips off his fur under the dripping tap in our kitchen sink; Tetanus, the hairdresser's thick-set black, who took a fancy to sleep on top of our china-cupboard all one winter, and used to startle me very much by jumping down heavily on to my shoulder as I made the breakfast coffee; Sweet Charity, a little grey Persian who came to a sad end under the wheels of a police-car; Charity's grey-and-white stripey cousin Fred, whose owners presently moved from next door to another part of the town.

It was soon after Fred's departure that Humblepuppy arrived, and from my point of view he couldn't have been more welcome. Taffy missed Fred badly, and expected *me* to play with him instead; it was sad to see this large elderly tabby rushing hopefully up and down the stairs after breakfast, or hiding behind the armchair and jumping out on to nobody; or howling, howling, howling at me until I escorted him out into the garden, where he'd rush to the lavender-bush which had been the traditional hiding-place of Whisky, Tetanus, Charity and Fred in succession. Cats have their habits and histories, just the same as humans.

So sometimes, on a working morning, I'd be at my wits' end, almost on the point of going across the town to our ex-neighbours, ringing their bell, and saying, 'Please can Fred come and play?' Specially on a rainy, uninviting day when Taffy was pacing gloomily about the house with drooping head and switching tail, grumbling about the weather and the lack of company, and blaming me for both.

Humblepuppy's arrival changed all that.

At first Taffy considered it necessary to police him, and that kept him fully occupied for hours. He'd sit on guard by the deedbox till Humblepuppy woke up in the morning, and then he'd follow officiously all over the house, wherever the visitor went. Humblepuppy was slow and cautious in his explorations, but by degrees he picked up courage and found his way into every corner. He never once made a puddle; he learned to use Taffy's cat-flap and go out into the garden, though he was always more timid outside and would scamper for home at any loud noise. Planes and cars terrified him, he never became used to them; which made me still more certain that he had been in that deedbox for a long, long time since before such things were invented.

Presently he learned, or Taffy taught him, to hide in the lavender-bush like Whisky, Charity, Tetanus, and Fred; and the two of them used to play their own ghostly version of touch-last for hours on end while I got on with my typing.

When visitors came, Humblepuppy always retired to his deedbox; he was decidedly scared of strangers; which made his behaviour with Mr Manningham, the new rector of Riverland, all the more surprising.

I was dying to learn anything I could of the old rectory's history, so I'd invited Mr Manningham to tea.

He was a thin, gentle, quiet man, who had done missionary work in the Far East and fell ill and had to come back to England. He seemed a little sad and lonely; said he still missed his Far East friends and work. I liked him. He told me that for a large part of the nineteenth century the Riverland living had belonged to a parson called Swannett, the Reverend Timothy Swannett, who lived to a great age and had ten children.

'He was a great-uncle of mine, as a matter of fact. But why do you want to know all this?' Mr Manningham asked. His long thin arm hung over the side of his chair; absently he moved his hand sideways and remarked, 'I didn't notice that you had a puppy.' Then he looked down and said 'Oh!'

'He's never come out for a stranger before,' I said.

Taffy, who maintains a civil reserve with visitors, sat motionless on the nightstore heater, eyes slitted, sphinxlike.

Humblepuppy climbed invisibly on to Mr Manningham's lap.

We agreed that the new rector probably carried a familiar smell of the rectory with him; or possibly he reminded Humblepuppy of his great-uncle, the Rev. Swannett.

Anyway, after that, Humblepuppy always came scampering joyfully out if Mr Manningham dropped in to tea, so of course I thought of the rector when summer holiday time came round.

During the summer holidays we lend our house and cat to a lady publisher and her mother who are devoted to cats and think it a privilege to look after Taffy and spoil him. He is always amazingly overweight when we get back. But the old lady has an allergy to dogs, and is frightened of them too; it was plainly out of the question that she should be expected to share her summer holiday with the ghost of a puppy.

So I asked Mr Manningham if he'd be prepared to take Humblepuppy as a boarder, since it didn't seem a case for the usual kind of boarding-kennels; he said he'd be delighted.

I drove Humblepuppy out to Riverland in his deedbox; he was rather miserable on the drive, but luckily it is not far. Mr Manningham came into the garden to meet us. We put the box down on the lawn and opened it.

I've never heard a puppy so wildly excited. Often I'd been sorry that I couldn't see Humblepuppy, but I was never sorrier than on that afternoon, as we heard him rushing from tree to familiar tree, barking joyously, dashing through the orchard grass—you could see it divide as he whizzed along—coming back to bounce up against us, all damp and earthy and smelling of leaves.

'He's going to be happy with you, all right,' I said, and Mr Manningham's grey, lined face, crinkled into its thoughtful smile as he said, 'It's the place more than me, I think.'

Well, it was both of them really.

After the holiday, I went to collect Humblepuppy, leaving

Taffy haughty and standoffish, sniffing our cases. It always takes him a long time to forgive us for going away.

Mr Manningham had a bit of a cold and was sitting by the fire in his study, wrapped in a shetland rug. Humblepuppy was on his knee. I could hear the little dog's tail thump against the arm of the chair when I walked in, but he didn't get down to greet me. He stayed in Mr Manningham's lap.

'So you've come to take back my boarder,' Mr Manningham said.

There was nothing in the least strained about his voice or smile but—I just hadn't the heart to take back Humblepuppy. I put my hand down, found his soft wrinkly forehead, rumpled it a bit, and said,

'Well—I was sort of wondering: our spoilt old cat seems to have got used to being on his own again; I was wondering whether— by any chance—you'd feel like keeping him?'

Mr Manningham's face lit up. He didn't speak for a minute; then he put a gentle hand down to find the small head, and rubbed a finger along Humblepuppy's chin.

'Well,' he said. He cleared his throat. 'Of course, if you're *quite* sure—'

'Quite sure.' My throat needed clearing too.

'I hope you won't catch my cold,' Mr Manningham said. I shook my head and said, 'I'll drop in to see if you're better in a day or two,' and went off and left them together.

Poor Taffy was pretty glum over the loss of his playmate for several weeks; we had two hours' purgatory every morning after breakfast while he hunted for Humblepuppy high and low. But gradually the memory faded and, thank goodness, now he has found a new friend, Little Grey Furry, a nephew, cousin or other relative of Charity and Fred. Little Grey Furry has learned to play hide-and-seek in the lavender-bush, and to use our cat-flap, and clean up whatever is in Taffy's food bowl, so all is well in that department.

But I still miss Humblepuppy. I miss his cold nose exploring the palm of my hand, as I sit thinking, in the middle of a page, and his warm weight leaning against my knee as he watches the commercials. And the scritch-scratch of his toenails on the dining-room floor and the flump, flump, as he comes downstairs, and the small hollow in a cushion as he settles down with a sigh.

Oh well, I'll get over it, just as Taffy has. But I was wondering about putting an ad. into *Our Dogs* or *Pets' Monthly*: Wanted, ghost of mongrel puppy. Warm welcome, loving home. Any reasonable price paid.

It might be worth a try.

From *A Harp of Fishbones* by Joan Aiken
(Jonathan Cape)
(See Note, page 155)

How the Lizard Fought the Leopard

A Story from Sri Lanka

Once upon a time in a certain forest, there lived a leopard.

One evening the leopard went out hunting as usual. He looked for a deer, or a pig, or even a small hare, but he found nothing, big or small. He was very hungry.

At last he met a lizard.

The leopard said: 'You shall be my dinner tonight, Lizard.'

The lizard said: 'Sir, I am not big enough for your meal. Please let me go.'

The leopard said: 'No, I shall not let you go. A mouthful is better than nothing for a hungry person.'

The lizard said: 'I have no sharp teeth like you; I have no strong claws like you. You are strong and I am weak. The strong should not kill the weak. It isn't fair. It is not the Dharma of our country.'

The leopard said impatiently: 'The weak always talk of the Dharma. The strong know only one law—"Might is right". I have might; so I have the right to kill you.'

The lizard said: 'Very well, I am ready to die, but I'll die fighting.'

At this the leopard laughed loudly. 'I fight only with my equals,' he roared.

'Very well,' said the lizard, 'give me three months and I'll be your equal.'

The leopard agreed and they decided that they would meet again at that very place, at that very hour, when the three months were over.

Now the lizard began to get ready for the fight. Every day he went to the rice fields and rolled himself in the mud. Then he washed his face and hands and sat in the sun until the mud dried on his body. He did this daily for three months. Thus he became bigger and bigger and fatter and fatter, until he was a giant lizard.

At the end of three months, the leopard and the lizard met at the very same place, at the very same hour. The fight began. The leopard sprang forward and struck the lizard with his paw again and again. At each blow a cake of mud fell off the lizard's back, but the lizard was unhurt.

The lizard in turn jumped on the leopard's back and bit the leopard's ears and eyes and nose and forehead. He bit the leopard's body all over. Now the leopard was bleeding. Blood flowed from his ears and eyes and nose and forehead. Blood flowed from every part of his body. Still the lizard went on biting. The leopard's body was covered with wounds. He could not bear the pain any longer. With a loud cry, he ran as fast as he could from the battlefield.

The poor defeated leopard sat under a tree. He looked over his right shoulder and felt it with his paw. There was a wound there. 'That lizard bit me here,' he moaned. He looked over his left shoulder and felt it with his paw. There was a wound there too. 'And he bit me here,' he groaned. With his paw he felt his ears, his eyes, his nose and his forehead and his back. There were wounds everywhere. He kept on repeating: 'He bit me here, and he bit me here, and he bit me here. He bit me all over.'

Now the leopard did not know that there was a woodcutter up in the tree. This man had seen the fight and heard the leopard's words and seen the leopard's wounds. He wanted to laugh. It was such a funny sight—a huge leopard sitting under a tree and crying over the wounds caused by a small lizard! At last he could control himself no longer and he burst into a loud 'Ha!Ha!Ha!'

The leopard looked up and saw the woodcutter. Had he been watched? He was angry because he didn't want anyone to know about his defeat. He climbed up the tree and snarled: 'Stop your "Ha!Ha!Ha!" or I'll eat you here and now.'

'Oh, sir, please pardon me and spare my life!' implored the woodcutter.

'But you know my secret and for that reason you must die,' roared the leopard.

'I swear by the gods of this forest that I'll keep the secret,' said the woodcutter.

The leopard said: 'That is not enough. You must swear by your wife that you won't tell her the secret. You must swear by your children that you won't tell them the secret.' And the woodcutter swore by his wife and children. The leopard was still not satisfied. 'What about the other villagers?' he said. 'You might tell them.'

'I swear by the Buddha that I won't tell the secret to anyone in the village,' said the woodcutter. So the leopard allowed the man to go back to his village.

The leopard himself lay in his den, licking his wounds. He was still worried, for he thought: 'These two-legged creatures are not to be trusted. I am sure that rascal the woodcutter will tell his wife the secret. When a woman knows a secret it is no longer a secret. I must go this very night and find out whether the man has kept his word.' The leopard hurried to the back yard of the woodcutter's hut, crouched against the wall, and listened to the sounds in the house.

The woodcutter and his wife and their children were seated on a mat eating their dinner of rice and vegetables. Suddenly the woodcutter broke into peals of laughter.

'Father, why are you laughing?' asked the children.

'Sh-ssh. It's a secret,' said their father.

'Father, please tell us the secret so that we can laugh too,' begged his daughter.

'No! No! I must not tell it to anyone. I have sworn by the Buddha,' replied her father.

The meal went on. Again the father began to laugh.

The woodcutter's wife said: 'Children, your father must be mad. There, he has choked himself with his rice through laughing!' She slapped him hard on the back and held a cup of water to his mouth.

After dinner, the children went to their mats and were soon asleep. The woodcutter stretched himself on his rattan bed and his wife lay on her mat in the corner. But sleep did not come to the woodcutter or his wife. Every time he closed his eyes he felt he must laugh. His wife could not sleep either until she knew her husband's secret. Again the woodcutter went 'Ha!Ha!Ha!'

The woman sat up on her mat. 'What is it? Won't you tell me your secret now?' she asked. 'The children are all asleep and no one will hear us.'

The man said: 'I have sworn to tell the secret to no one, not even to you.'

However, the woman went on pleading until her husband gave in. He told her how he had seen the fight between the leopard and the lizard and how the lizard had won. 'Then,' he said, 'the leopard came to lie down under my tree and kept saying:'' That lizard bit me here! He bit me here! He bit me all over!'' '

'Ha!Ha!Ha!' His wife joined in the laughter.

All this while the leopard had been crouching against the wall listening. He had heard the woodcutter's maddening 'Ha!Ha!Ha!' and now he heard the woman's laughter as well. He was furious. He waited until the man and the woman fell asleep; then he leaped on to the roof of the hut. He removed part of the rice-straw thatch and slid into the loft. From there he lowered himself into the kitchen and opened the back door. Then he crept under the rattan bed, lifted it on to his back with the man still asleep, and walked out by the back door.

It was not until the leopard had reached the forest that the woodcutter awoke. He felt the bed moving. The moon had just risen and through the holes in the rattan bed he saw the black spots on the leopard's back. He knew that the leopard was out for his blood and he was terrified. Just then he caught sight of an overhanging branch of a big tree. In a flash he grasped it and lifted himself up into the tree.

Unaware of what was happening, the leopard went on. He reached the mouth of his den and put the bed down. But where was the rascally woodcutter? Grumbling, the leopard went back to look for him. There in the moonlight he saw the woodcutter sitting in the tree. Without a word, the leopard dug his claws into the trunk and began to climb. The woodcutter was very wide awake by this time. He shouted: 'Mr Leopard, if you love your life, climb no further. There's a lizard just above me and he's waiting to bite you!'

Hearing the word lizard, the terrified leopard leaped from the tree and ran away as fast as he could. In a moment he had disappeared from sight. And the woodcutter returned home still laughing 'Ha!Ha!Ha!'

That was the last the woodcutter or anyone else saw of the leopard. They say he crossed the hills and hid his shame in a distant forest where there were no lizards or woodcutters.

From *Folk Tales from Asia. Vol.2* by E. R. Eratne
Edited by Eileen Colwell and Kyoke Matsuoka
(See Note, page 156)

Peter's Mermaid

Peter MacAuslan was very fond of his old Aunt Em; there was something about her that seemed to make nice things happen. His parents were fond of her too but, being very tidy and particular themselves, they disapproved of her because she was not. 'Those purple cardigans!' they said to each other. 'That bird's-nest hair! And why must she always carry that dreadful old shopping bag that smells of fish—surely she can't always be shopping, for she certainly hasn't got much money!'

But Peter liked her being untidy and he often used to go and stay with her in her nice shabby cottage with a stream in the garden which ran down to the sea. She never minded crabs on the carpet or sand in the bath, or asked silly questions, and he could feed the sea-gulls on her kitchen window-sill and play draughts with Aunt Em in the evenings.

Sometimes Aunt Em came up and stayed with Peter and his family and he liked that very much too. There was something calm about Aunt Em. If Peter got into trouble she never sided with the grown-ups just because she *was* one. She didn't say very

27

much at all. She just sat there, nice and solid.

One Sunday afternoon, when his Aunt Em was staying with him, Peter went fishing in the river near his house. He spent the whole of the afternoon wading about in the dirty water, until his feet were quite numb with cold, and he caught nothing at all. Very few people went down to that part of the river now because it was too near the town to be nice any more and even the fish had moved away. It had rusty tins in it and beer bottles and old pram wheels and scavenging dogs.

It was just when he was about to pack up his things and go home that he felt his net drag down in his hands. It was so heavy that he very nearly broke the stick part, bringing it to land. When Peter saw gleaming silver scales and a waving tail he thought he had got a huge fish all matted up with black weed and it wasn't until he had tipped it out on the bank that he realized he had caught a baby mermaid with long dark hair. Fancy!

'I can't believe it!' Peter said to himself. 'My brain must have gone numb as well as my feet!' But there was no doubt about it; two watery blue eyes stared up at him out of a round pink face, and there was a very small mouth which opened and shut. *'Gosh!'* said Peter, gazing at his catch with pride and delight. *'Well!* My *goodness!'* The mermaid looked trustful but said nothing. 'All I can say *is,'* said Peter breathlessly, 'what a bit of *luck!'*

He rolled her up in his raincoat, because somehow the little mermaid looked so very cold and bare (though of course you can't always go by appearances, and it is ever so much colder at the bottom of a river than it is on dry land). Then he carried her back to his house, and she wrapped her little soft wet hands round his neck and twined her frog-fingers in his hair, and breathed her cold breath on his cheek, very confidingly.

Now, a long time ago, when Peter MacAuslan had been a very little boy, and Aunt Em had been staying with him then too, he had caught a field-mouse and brought it home and Aunt Em had found him a box to put it in. But when he showed it to his mother she had made him let it go in the field at the bottom of the garden although he had terribly, terribly wanted to keep it. Now Peter wanted even more terribly still to keep the baby mermaid, so he decided not to risk showing her to his mother, but tiptoed as quietly as he could upstairs into his bedroom and dumped her down on his chair. He offered her one of his old picture books to look at while he went down to supper, and she took it, smiling very nicely.

'If you had a mermaid,' said Peter, sitting very bolt-upright and excited in the dining-room, 'what would you call her?'

'Amaryllis,' said his Aunt Em.

But Peter's mother looked worried. 'What a strange thing to say!' she murmured to her husband, 'and he looks so flushed and bright-eyed. I'm afraid he may be sickening for measles. I hear there is a lot about just now.'

She watched him so anxiously that it was all Peter could do to slip a few things from his plate into his pocket for Amaryllis to eat, and afterwards his mother absolutely insisted on coming upstairs with him so that she could take his temperature and tuck him into bed with a hot water bottle. Peter ran on ahead of her to try to hide the mermaid and he just had time to seize her and push her under the bed, where she remained as quiet as a mouse, with one eye peering between the fringes of his counterpane.

'Why, what in the world have you been doing to your bedroom!' cried Mrs MacAuslan.

Peter looked round. The mermaid seemed to be very inquisitive. She had not stayed in her chair looking quietly at her picture book but had spent suppertime slipping and slithering all round the room, leaving great pools of water and looking into all the drawers and cupboards. She had also emptied the water-jug over herself. Even the curtains were crumpled and wet where she had climbed up them to look out of the window.

Peter tried hard to think of some good reason why his bedroom should be looking like that and his face got redder still as it always did when he was even *thinking* of telling a story, because he was such a very honest boy, and his mother looked at him in concern.

'Well, never mind, dear. We will say no more about it this time because you really do look quite feverish. Hop into bed and I will bring you up some hot milk. But remember, I never want to see your room looking like this again, or I shall be very angry indeed. What can you have been thinking of!' And Mrs MacAuslan flicked the counterpane off the bed so sharply that some of the fringes caught Amaryllis in the eye and made her squeak, and Peter had to bounce about on his bed and pretend it was the squeaky springs.

When his mother had gone down he pulled out the mermaid and told her that she mustn't make his bedroom so wet and untidy and she looked at him sadly with eyes full of tears, so he gave her a sausage and a banana to cheer her up. It was difficult to be cross with that mermaid somehow. Then he noticed that her skin was very dry and he kept glancing round looking for some more water and he was just wondering what to do about it when there was a knock on the door and there was Aunt Em come in to say goodnight and ask if there was anything she could get him. 'Yes please,' said Peter. 'A bucket of water, if it wouldn't be too much trouble.'

So Aunt Em, who never asked unnecessary questions, went straight downstairs and fetched him one out of the kitchen. When she came back with the bucket she caught sight of Amaryllis under the bed. 'Oh, there's your mermaid!' she said, smiling kindly. 'What a dear little thing she is, to be sure!' Then Aunt Em kissed Peter goodnight and Amaryllis curled up in the bucket and went to sleep.

The next morning Peter got up and told his mother that he felt quite all right and hadn't got the measles after all, and then he took his bike and rode off to see his friend David Chetwynd, taking Amaryllis with him in his bicycle basket.

David was very interested to meet a real mermaid and he suggested that they kept her in the goldfish pond in his garden. Mr Chetwynd was a keen gardener and he had made the pool very cleverly, with irises and rockeries and waterlilies and even a bridge which looked very charming though it was really only strong enough for the birds to walk on. The mermaid liked that idea and she slipped into the pool at once because she had felt much too dry in the bicycle basket.

The boys watched her swimming in the pool amongst the goldfish for quite a long time and then they left some breakfast on the bank for her and started off for school as quickly as they could because they were rather late, and it was lucky that they met David's father on the way to his office and he gave them a lift in his car or they would have been even later.

Peter and David could hardly wait for break so that they could talk about Amaryllis, but they didn't tell the other boys because they were afraid that their parents might find out if too many people knew about it, and they might even make them put Amaryllis back in the river and she would be eaten by the dogs and cut by the tins and bottles and get her long hair tangled up with the pram wheels. At lunchtime they saved as much food as they could and put it in their handkerchiefs and after school was over they hurried back to David's garden.

Amaryllis was very pleased to see them. She was sitting on the bank beside a little fire, looking very cheerful and innocent. But, oh dear, she had knocked down the tiny bridge and built herself a house with the stones, and she had picked all the irises to thatch the roof and, worst of all, she was just roasting the last of the poor goldfish. David Chetwynd turned quite pale. 'Oh, my giddy gosh!' he whispered. 'My father will be *wild*!'

Peter was angry with Amaryllis and he picked her up and was about to give her a good shake when she looked up at him with such round blue eyes that he hadn't the heart. 'She doesn't mean to be naughty,' he said. 'Mermaids do eat fish, you know, and surely it's just as good to have a house as a bridge, if you look at it that way. After all, not many people are lucky enough to have a real mermaid's house in their goldfish pool, are they?'

'N-no,' agreed David doubtfully. 'But that's all very well, just try explaining it to Dad. You'd just better get her out of here before he comes home, that's all!'

So Peter picked up Amaryllis rather wearily and carried her back to his own house in the bicycle basket, riding very slowly. His Aunt Em was sunning herself in the back garden.

'We're back again,' he said, and he stared thoughtfully at the little mermaid, who looked back at him very kindly with her watery blue eyes. 'H'm—I really can't think quite what to do with her,' confessed Peter, who suddenly remembered he had not done any homework. Everything seemed to be very difficult. 'I can't put her back in the dirty old river. It's not at all suitable for her. It's full of broken glass. I do so want to keep her, but how can I?'

'Well . . .' said Aunt Em slowly. 'Well . . . let me see now. By the way, where is she?'

Peter looked round. Amaryllis had disappeared. Oh dear, she really *was* a worry! He and Aunt Em searched in the flowerbeds. 'I do hope she hasn't gone out into the road,' he said. 'She doesn't understand about traffic. She might be run over.'

'Oh no, of course not, dear, she couldn't have,' replied his aunt comfortably. 'She was here just a minute ago. She can't be far away.'

They both looked all over the house and then they looked all over the garden again but they couldn't find so much as a single silver scale. Peter's mother came out of the back door. 'Has Aunt Em gone?' she called to him. 'She never said goodbye to me.'

'No, here I am,' said Aunt Em, 'I'm just off, dear.'

'Oh, but you are late,' said Mrs MacAuslan. 'You will miss your train, Aunt Em. I'll fetch you a taxi.' And she ran out of the front gate, thinking how very vague and absent-minded dear old Aunt Em was becoming.

'I'd forgotten about your train,' said Peter.

'Yes, I'd better go, dear,' said his aunt, 'otherwise it will look peculiar. Amaryllis is probably hiding somewhere you know, having a game with us. I'm sure you'll find her soon. I'll ring you up tonight and find out what has happened.'

But when Aunt Em telephoned it was to say that when she got out of the taxi at the station she had found Amaryllis herself, curled up fast asleep in her shopping bag, 'It smells so nice and fishy you know, just what she would like. I ought to have thought of that.'

Peter's smile of relief gradually faded. He wrinkled his brow.

What now? He would have to go and fetch her of course. He tried to remember how much money he had in his money-box; four shillings was it, or four and sixpence? Not enough, he felt sure, for the train fare. And how should he explain his journey at home? And then, when he had got her, what should he do with her? He loved Amaryllis dearly but there was no denying, she was quite a handful.

'Do you want her back, dear, or shall I keep her with me down here?'

Peter hesitated. 'Do you want her?' he asked.

'Oh yes, I should love her and she's such a help. She's putting shells all round the edges of my flowerbeds already and it looks so pretty. And of course there's the sea for her to swim in.'

'Can I bring David down to see her sometimes?'

'Of course you can. Any time you like.'

So Amaryllis lives very happily down by the shore, with Aunt Em. In the daytime she often goes far far out to sea but she always swims back upstream in the evenings when the lamps are lit in the little cottage, and taps on the door. Sometimes she has a present for Aunt Em, a piece of rock-crystal perhaps, or gems from the bed of the sea, or bits of furniture from long-forgotten shipwrecks. Then they will settle down in front of the fire for a game of draughts together. And whenever Peter and David go down to spend a weekend with them, Amaryllis takes that old shopping bag out to sea and brings it back full of shrimps or oysters, for a very special supper.

Mr and Mrs MacAuslan are most surprised when they go down to the cottage nowadays. 'Aunt Em can't be so badly off. Surely those were real pearls she was wearing,' they tell each other. 'And she used to be so untidy, but just look at her garden now. It is really most artistic in an unusual kind of way. Very strange of course but isn't that just like Aunt Em!'

From *Charlotte Hough's Holiday Book*
by Charlotte Hough (Heinemann)
(See Note, page 157)

Prot and Krot

There was once a soldier who had been away from Poland for many years fighting in the war with Sweden. When the war was over he took a ship for home and it cost him nearly all his money. By the time he arrived at the port of Danzig, he had only two coins in his pocket, a small loaf of bread in his knapsack, and nothing else.

His home was in the south near Sandomiersh, by the river Vistula, and he thought he would follow the river on foot, since he could not afford to sail or ride.

He had not gone far when he came to a churchyard where two old men sat together on a bench. They looked at the soldier as he passed by.

'Hello there, fine soldier boy!' one of them called. 'God be with you.'

'And with you,' answered the soldier, raising his cap.

34

'Tell us, laddie, where you have been soldiering?' asked the second old man.

The soldier was anxious to be on his way, but he was a civil fellow, so he stopped out of politeness. 'I've been in many places, fighting the Swedes,' he said. 'Now I'm on my way home to Sandomiersh.'

'Ah, it must be good to have a home to go to,' said the first old man. 'Some people have all the luck in the world. My name is Prot, and this is my brother Krot.'

'Yes, yes, I'm Krot and he's Prot. At least we think so, but we're never quite sure. Anyway, what does it matter? Our trouble is that we have neither home, food, nor even a penny between us.'

'Well, I've only two pennies left,' said the soldier, drawing the coins from his purse. 'You can have them if they're any use to you.' He gave the money to the old men, and their eyes twinkled with merriment as they exchanged looks.

'We won't forget you, soldier boy,' they said. 'It's good to know there's a little kindness left in the world.'

The soldier saluted his elders and went on his way, whistling gaily. It was a long walk to Sandomiersh, and after travelling for many hours he felt tired and hungry. His old boots had trodden many battlefields and they were now so full of holes that he could hardly walk in them.

'A bite of bread's the order of the day now, I think,' he said to himself, taking the rye bread from his knapsack. He was about to cut off a piece with his knife when he heard someone calling him.

'Hello there, soldier boy!'

The soldier turned his head in the direction of the river, from where the voice came, and there he saw Prot and Krot floating past on a simple raft made of bits of wood tied together with rope.

He gave them a wave, then noticed something quite extraordinary about the raft. It was moving upstream, against the current—without help from anyone! The soldier hurried alongside and called out:'Where did you find such a raft?'

'Oh, here and there. Bits and pieces we bought with the money you gave us,' Prot called back.

'That's right, bits and pieces,' echoed Krot. 'We're still hungry. Have you got anything to eat?'

'Only a small loaf,' answered the soldier. 'You're welcome to share it.'

'Then jump aboard. We're going your way as you see,' said Prot.

'Going your way,' said Krot.

So the soldier jumped on the raft, and the three of them shared the bread, which was very little indeed, and they had nothing to drink. But the old men did not complain. They were surprisingly good companions.

'Tell us, soldier boy, what would you wish for if you could have anything in the world?' asked Prot.

'Ah, that would take a lot of thought,' replied the soldier, tapping his pipe to clean it out a bit. 'There's not much in the world I really need.'

'Surely there must be something,' insisted Prot. 'Treasure and a fine manor house, perhaps?'

'Oooooooh yes! Treasure and a manor house,' said Krot.

'No, no, nothing like that. I wouldn't know how to be a grand gentleman. No, thank you, but I'd like a nice pipeful of tobacco and perhaps a few coins in my purse. That would satisfy me, I think,' said the soldier.

'Go on, soldier boy, think harder,' urged Prot. 'Anything in the world.'

'Yes, much harder. Anything at all,' said Krot.

The soldier touched the knapsack with his foot. 'Well,' he said slowly,' since I don't want to own much more than a knapsack, it would be useful if it could hold anything, or even anyone, just for the asking. What do you think of that?'

'Not bad, not bad,' said Prot.

'Not bad,' said Krot. 'Such wishes might come true.'

'Oh yes,' laughed the soldier. 'Like pie in the sky, or wine in the brine, no doubt.'

No sooner had he spoken than a big round pie appeared in the sky over their heads. Down it came and settled itself on the raft;

shiny brown, crusty and filled with tender beef and vegetables. At the same time, in the water there appeared three bottles of red wine, knocking themselves against the raft as though begging to be opened.

Prot and Krot and the soldier ate the delicious pie, and washed it down with a bottle of red wine each. The soldier was astonished by the appearance of the food and drink, but he was so hungry, he ate first and thought to ask questions afterwards. As they finished their meal, the raft was nearing Sandomiersh.

'Time for you to get off, said Prot.

'Yes, off you go,' said Krot.

The soldier picked up his knapsack and leapt on to the green bank. 'Goodbye and thank you,' he called back. 'But do tell me where . . .' He looked up and down the river, but there was no raft to be seen and no Prot and Krot. The expanse of the Vistula was empty, save for a heron diving low over the water, and a kingfisher waiting motionless on a log.

'Such things could only happen in a dream,' muttered the soldier, rubbing his eyes. 'I must have been walking in my sleep.'

He slung his small pack over his shoulder and put his pipe in his mouth, although there was no tobacco in it. As he sucked away absentmindedly, the pipe began to smoke, and the scent of sweet tobacco came from the bowl.

'Heavens above! Prot and Krot!' cried the soldier, looking about him as though he expected the two old men to be lurking in the grass. 'Wherever you are, I thank you for your kindness.' There was no sound in the quiet countryside, but the smoke from the pipe shaped itself into words which spelled out:

'YOUR KINDNESS IS REWARDED.'

The soldier went on his way wondering who the strange old men could be. By evening he came to an inn where he thought he would ask for a drink of water, since he had no money for anything else. As he walked through the doorway, the purse in his belt began to feel heavier and heavier. On opening it he found that it was full of gold pieces! He ate a good supper of boiled beef in horseradish sauce, and cheese pancakes, and as he took a coin from his purse to pay the innkeeper, another one immediately came in its place. His second wish had come true!

Now the soldier did not know it, but sitting near him was a robber who saw the gold and made up his mind to have the purse. He waited in a dark corner outside the inn, ready to spring. When the soldier came out, night had fallen and before he knew what was happening the robber jumped out and demanded the money.

'My money?' said the surprised soldier.

'That's it! The gold in your purse. I saw it and I'll have it, or I'll have your life,' snarled the robber.

The soldier thought quickly about his third wish, which might, only *might*, just come true. He decided to try it.

'I have put the purse in my knapsack,' he said. 'Take it by all means.' Swinging his pack to the ground, he unfastened the buckle. As the robber bent down, the soldier said: 'Into my knapsack and stay there.'

As quick as lightning, the robber shot head first into the knapsack and was stuck fast. The soldier hoisted him on to his back and tipped him into the well in front of the inn.

'*Splash!*' Down he went to the bottom, and the soldier wound down the rope and the bucket. 'Sit in the bucket,' he shouted. 'Someone may pull you up, if you're lucky,' and away he went.

The night was warm and the sky was bright with a sprinkling of stars. The soldier took the road home which ran close to the castle of the king. He remembered how as a boy he used to watch hundreds of candles flickering in the windows and wonder what the royal family was doing.

Shortly before he reached the castle walls he saw a curious sight in a turnip field. There among the ripe turnips stood a round golden tent, guarded by a circle of the king's guards. On the hill above rose the royal castle without a single light shining in any of its windows. The soldier thought this strange and stopped to inquire.

'What's wrong?' he asked. 'The castle looks deserted.'

'So it is and likely to be for many a year,' said one of the guards. 'His Majesty can no longer live there.'

'But why?' asked the soldier.

'Surely everyone in these parts knows by now that the castle is haunted by a demon that will not give the king peace, day or night. No one can get rid of it, no one at all, and the king can bear it no more.'

'I think perhaps I may be able to help the king,' said the soldier obligingly.

'I would be indebted to you all my life if you could,' said the king, emerging from his tent in his nightgown.

The astonished soldier fell upon his knees. 'Your Majesty, let me go to the castle tonight before I return home, and I will rid you of the demon.'

'My dear fellow,' said the king, straightening his nightcap, 'you don't know what you are saying. You, go there alone, when I and all my courtiers could not bear it? No, no, it is too much to ask. I cannot allow it.'

'Perhaps Your Majesty is fond of camping out?' ventured the soldier.

'Not in the least, dear boy! It's so unroyal, don't you see? And most uncomfortable,' replied the king, patting his aching back.

'Then let me help, I only ask permission to sleep in the castle tonight, that's all.'

The king could hardly refuse. He went into his tent, and returned with a huge key. 'There you are,' he said. 'This key will open the door. Go if you must, and if you succeed, you may have any part of my kingdom you wish as a reward.'

The soldier thanked the king, took the key and went up the hill to the darkened castle. He put the key in the lock and let himself into the main hall, where he thought he would spend the night. Taking off his jacket, he put it under his head, and with his knapsack close beside him, he lay down to sleep.

He had scarcely closed his eyes when he was awakened by a shrieking and howling, and a thin high voice calling in the darkness: 'Get out! Get out! This is my castle. Everybody out! Clear the way, clear the way. Not even a mouse is allowed to stay. *It is all mine!*'

The soldier opened his eyes, and by the light of the moon, he saw a small figure prancing about. It seemed to be dressed in black, with pointed ears, pointed nose and long pointed toes. As it went about lifting its knees up to its chin, it saw the figure of the soldier in the corner.

'I said everybody out!' screamed the demon. 'Out of here this instant, do you hear? *Out! Out! Out!*'

The soldier was not at all afraid. 'Why should I get out?' he said yawning. 'The king has given me permission to sleep here.'

'This is my castle now,' replied the demon, bouncing up on to the mantelpiece and glaring down at the soldier. 'If you don't go I'll—I'll turn you into a fly.'

'Then I'll buzz up and down your long nose,' said the soldier, lying down again as if he didn't care.

'Will you then, you impudent creature! In that case I'll turn you into a beetle,' yelled the demon, stamping up and down on the mantelpiece.

The soldier simply stretched himself and said casually:

'What a pleasure it will be for me then to nip all your long pointed toes.'

'*What!!!* I'll turn you into a . . . a . . . a . . .'

But before the demon could think of anything else to say, the soldier stood up and said quickly: 'I'll turn *you* into my knapsack this very instant and you will remain there until I let you go.'

Whizz! With the speed of an arrow the demon shot off the mantelpiece, straight into the knapsack, and the soldier fastened the buckle!

'Let me out of here, whoever you are!' the demon cried.

The soldier took no notice. He put the knapsack under his jacket, put his head down on the jacket and went to sleep. He was so tired that even the violent kicking of the demon did not disturb him.

In the morning the king sent a troop of his guards to find out what had happened to the brave soldier. The men peered through the window and saw the soldier sitting on his small pack, peacefully smoking his pipe. Still they did not dare to go in, so they tapped on the window and shouted:

'Are you all right?'

'I'm very well, thank you,' replied the soldier.

'Did you see the demon?'

'Yes, of course I did,' said the soldier, blowing smoke rings.

'Where is it now?' asked the soldiers, fearfully glancing about them.

'Why, I'm sitting on it,' answered the soldier. 'Now no more questions if you please. Go and bring me forty blacksmiths with hammers and a barrel of wine.'

'*Bring what?*' gasped the soldiers.

'You heard me. Quickly, do as I say.' The soldier was beginning to lose patience with the frightened men. Away galloped the guards and they returned two hours later with forty blacksmiths in a cart, and behind them a wagon containing forty hammers and a barrel of wine.

The soldier ordered the blacksmiths to take it in turns hammering on his knapsack, which they did without knowing why. When they were thirsty they took a drink from the barrel, then hammered away with a will.

The demon in the knapsack began to squeal with terror. 'Stop it, stop it, d'you hear? You'll never hurt a demon with a hammer, or a hundred hammers, or a thousand hammers, or even a million hammers. Demons can't feel hammers—Ouch!'

'What did you say?' called the soldier above the noise.

'I said you'll never, *ouch!* Hurt me, *ouch!* Never, * oooo-heeyerooh!!!* Stop it, I can't bear it any more!' screeched the demon, who could indeed feel every single blow from the hammers.

'That's what His Majesty said about you,' shouted the soldier. 'If you promise to leave this land and never return, the hammering will stop. The king wishes to live at peace in his castle.'

For a moment the demon said nothing, then a few extra hard blows persuaded him.

'That's enough. I promise. I promise. Have mercy on me. Let me go and I'll never come back.'

The hammering stopped and the soldier opened his knapsack. 'Come out,' he said. A long black pointed toe emerged, then an arm, a long nose, and two green eyes looked out in fear.

'Hurry up before I change my mind,' said the soldier sternly.

At once the creature sprang up like a frog and ran away at top speed, down the hill and across the fields until it disappeared in the distance.

The soldier went to the king, who was eating breakfast rolls in his tent.

'You must be the bravest soldier in my entire kingdom,' he said when he heard the story.

'Not really, Your Majesty, only the most fortunate,' smiled the soldier, thinking of Prot and Krot.

'Say what you like, but I shall raise you to the rank of general. Not a word! It's the very least you deserve,' announced the king, offering a plate to the soldier. 'Have a roll, and put one in your pocket. Now I shall keep my promise to you. Tell me which part of my kingdom you would like for your own and it shall be yours.'

The soldier, who was not a greedy man, took only one roll and asked for very little. 'You are most kind, sire,' he said bowing. 'If it pleases Your Majesty, I need only the little cottage I already own, but if my land could reach down as far as the Vistula river, a matter of three hundred yards or so, then I would be more than content.'

'Ah ha! I see you are a fisherman at heart,' laughed the king. 'You are an easy man to please. I wish there were more like you. From this moment on, the land is yours with the Vistula as its border. And remember, you are most welcome at my castle whenever you wish to come.'

The soldier thanked the king, bowed again, and went home at last to his little cottage.

Every day he went to sit on the banks of the Vistula, not however to fish, as the king had thought. He puffed his pipe, which was always full of tobacco, and scanned the water for signs of a roughly made raft floating upstream, carrying Prot and Krot. He watched for many months and many years, but he never saw them again. He did not forget them, though, for they had given him all he needed to be happy for the rest of his life, and he lived to the age of one hundred and one!

From *The Amber Mountain and other folk stories*
by Agnes Szudek
(Hutchinson Junior Books)
(See Note, page 158)

The Gorgon's Head

Once upon a time in far away Greece there lived a youth named Perseus. His mother had been driven from her home by her cruel father and she and her little son were befriended by a kindly fisherman, Dictys, in the island of Seriphos. Here Perseus grew up until he was taller than any man in the island, and had great skill in running and wrestling, boxing and throwing the quoit, and all that befits a man.

But the king of the island was hard and cruel and because of the strength and beauty of Perseus, he longed to be rid of him. So he held a great feast to which he invited Perseus. Now it was the custom that every guest should bring a present, but Perseus had nothing to bring and stood at the gate of the palace, shamefaced and miserable. Then the king called him in and taunted him before all the guests. At last Perseus, mad with shame, cried out recklessly:

'Give me but time and I will bring you a nobler present than all these have given!'

'Hear him, hear the boaster! What is it to be?' jeered the guests.

'The head of the Gorgon,' cried Perseus, and there was silence

44

in the great hall. For the man who looked upon the Gorgon's head looked no more upon anything—he became a block of stone.

Then Perseus turned and strode out of the hall, his heart hot with anger—but cold with dread.

In his trouble Pallas Athene, the goddess, and Hermes, messenger of the gods, came to his help. Hermes gave him a pair of winged sandals to bear him over land and sea, and the sword, Argus-slayer, which kills at the first stroke. And so that he should not need to look upon the face of the Gorgon, Pallas Athene gave him a polished shield in which he might see the monster's image and aim his blow aright.

Then Perseus summoned up his courage and, shutting his eyes, leaped over the edge of the cliff into the empty air. Behold, instead of falling he floated and stood and ran along the sky, the sandals leading him ever northwards.

For many days he travelled, going dry-shod over land and sea, turning neither to the right hand nor the left, till he came to the Unshapen Land and the place which has no name.

Seven days he walked through it till he came to the edge of the everlasting night, where the air is full of feathers, and the soil hard with ice. There he found the Three Grey Sisters, nodding upon a white log of driftwood beneath the cold white winter moon.

There was no living thing around them, not a fly, not a sprig of moss upon the rocks. The surge broke up in foam, but it fell again in flakes of snow. The Sisters had but one eye between them, and one tooth, and though they passed the eye from one to another they could not see, and though they passed the tooth from one to the other, they could not eat.

And Perseus pitied them and said: 'Oh venerable mothers, tell me, if you can, the path to the Gorgon.'

Then one cried, 'This is the voice of one of the children of men.'

And another said, 'Give me the eye that I may see him.'

And another said, 'Give me the tooth so that I may bite him.'

Then Perseus stepped close to them and as they groped about between themselves, he held out his own hand and one of them

put the eye into it, fancying that it was the hand of her sister. Then he sprang back and cried: 'Cruel and proud old women, I have your eye. Unless you tell me the path to the Gorgon, I will throw it into the sea.'

Then they wept and chattered and scolded, but they were forced to tell the truth.

'You must go, foolish boy,' they said, 'to the Giant Atlas who holds the heavens and earth apart. And you must ask his daughters, the Hesperides, who are young and foolish like yourself.'

So Perseus gave them back their eye; but instead of using it, they nodded and fell fast asleep and were turned into blocks of ice, and the tide came up and washed them away. And now they float up and down for ever.

But Perseus sped away to the southward. The seagulls and the terns swept laughing over his head, while Perseus skimmed over the billows and leapt from wave to wave and was never weary. At last he saw, far away in the sunset, the Giant Atlas, his head amongst wreaths of clouds and his feet wrapped in forests.

On the shore Perseus heard sweet voices singing, for he had reached the Garden of the Hesperides, guardians of the tree that bears golden apples. He stepped forward and saw them dancing, hand in hand, round the tree with its gleaming fruit. And round the roots of the tree was coiled the snake that never sleeps, its forked tongue flickering in and out.

'Tell me, fair maidens,' said Perseus, 'the way which leads to the Gorgon, that I may go and slay her.'

Then they sighed and answered, 'Fair boy, we know not the way to the Gorgon, but we will ask the Giant Atlas for he can see far over the land and sea.'

So they all went up the mountain and found the giant kneeling as he held the heavens and earth apart. And Atlas said:

'I can see the Gorgon lying on an island far away, but you can never even go near her unless you have the cap of darkness, and that is in the regions of the dead. These maidens are immortal and shall fetch it for you if you will promise me one thing.'

46

Then Perseus promised and the giant said, 'When you come back with the Gorgon's head, show me the beautiful horror so that I may lose my feeling and breathing and become a stone for ever, for it is weary labour for me to hold the heavens and earth apart.'

Then one of the maidens went down into a dark cavern among the cliffs from which came smoke and thunder. For seven days Perseus and the nymphs waited trembling for her return. At last she came into the light again, her face pale with the horrors she had seen, but the magic cap in her hand.

Then Perseus put on the cap and vanished from their sight and went on boldly. Suddenly he heard the rustle of the Gorgon's wings and stopped short, his heart still with fear. For a while he hovered motionless, then rose into the air, his shield above his head to show him what lay below.

There far below him he saw the three Gorgons sleeping, two of them loathsome beasts, but the third with plumage like the rainbow and a face like a nymph. But her eyebrows were knit and her lips clenched with everlasting care and pain, and from among her tresses vipers' heads showed their fangs and hissed.

Then Perseus hesitated no longer, but swooped down like an eagle and, looking steadfastly into his shield, struck once—and needed not to strike again.

Then swiftly he wrapped the head in his cloak and sprang into the air faster than he had ever sprung before, for the other two Gorgons had awakened. Into the air they sprang yelling, on they rushed with a fearful howl, while the wind rattled in their wings. And Perseus' blood ran cold for all his courage and he cried, 'Bear me well, brave sandals, for the hounds of death are at my heels.'

And well the sandals bore him across the shoreless sea, and the Gorgons were outdistanced and Perseus sped swiftly towards the setting sun.

And so he came again to the Giant Atlas and the Garden of the Hesperides and he held the Gorgon's head so that Atlas might see it. Then the weary giant had rest and became a mighty mountain which sleeps for ever far above the clouds. Then Perseus bid the maidens farewell and sped across the trackless skies, lessening

47

and lessening like a seagull till they could see him no more.

For many days he journeyed and came at last to a land where the lowlands were drowned in floods and the highlands blasted with fire, and the hills heaved like a bubbling cauldron before the wrath of King Poseidon, the shaker of the earth.

All day Perseus flew along the shore by the sea and the sky was black with smoke and at night the sky was red with flame.

And at dawn he looked towards the cliffs and at the water's edge under a black rock, he saw a white image standing.

So he came near, but it was no statue but a maiden of flesh and blood. As he came closer still he could see how she shrank and shivered when the waves sprinkled her with cold salt spray. Her arms were spread above her head and fastened to the rock with chains of brass, and her head drooped with weariness and grief. She did not see Perseus for the cap of darkness was on his head.

Perseus was filled with pity and anger. 'I have never seen so beautiful a maiden,' he thought. 'Surely she is a king's daughter.'

He lifted the cap of darkness, so that he flashed into her sight. 'Do not fear me,' he cried. 'I will set you free.' He tore at her fetters, but they were too strong even for him.

'Touch me not!' warned the princess. 'I am doomed to be a sacrifice to the gods of the sea. Even if you can set me free, they will still slay me.'

'What dark fate has brought you here?' asked Perseus. 'Who are you?' and drawing the Argus-slayer he cut through the brass as if it had been flax.

'My name is Andromeda, and, alas, my life is to atone for my mother's boast that my beauty is greater than that of the Queen of the Sea. I am to be devoured by a sea monster, so that no other innocent blood shall be shed.'

'Not so!' said Perseus.'I have slain the beautiful horror, the Gorgon. Now the Gorgon's head shall help me to kill the monster. Hide your eyes lest the sight of the Gorgon freeze you into stone.'

'Look!' the maiden cried out in terror. 'There is the monster! Now I must die. Go, before you too are devoured.'

'It is the monster who will die!' said Perseus. 'Promise me that if

I slay the beast, you will be my wife and come back with me to my kingdom.'

And she promised, although with little hope.

Then Perseus laughed with joy and flew upward, while Andromeda crouched trembling on the rock.

On came the huge monster, coasting along like a black galley. His great sides were fringed with clustering shells and sea weed, and the water gurgled in and out of his wide jaws as he rolled along, dripping and glistening in the beams of the morning sun.

Then he saw Andromeda and shot forward to take his prey, while the waves foamed white behind him and before him the fish fled leaping.

Then down from the height of the air fell Perseus like a shooting star; down to the crest of the waves, while Andromeda hid her face. Then there was silence, and when at last she looked up, trembling, she saw Perseus springing towards her and instead of the monster there lay a long black rock with the sea rippling quietly round it.

Then the proud Perseus lifted Andromeda in his arms and flew with her to the cliff-top where stood her people. With harps and cymbals they welcomed the hero and for many days they feasted.

At last Perseus sailed home to Greece with his wife and there his mother and Dictys embraced him with joy, for it was seven years since he had departed on his quest and they had thought him dead.

With the Gorgon's head beneath a goatskin, Perseus entered the hall of the king, the man who had sent him on his fearful quest, thinking he would never return.

Perseus came into the hall. The king sat at the head of the table, his nobles and landowners on either side, feasting. Perseus stood on the threshold, but no one recognised him, for he had gone out a boy and now came home with the stature of a hero. His eyes shone like an eagle's and his beard was like a lion's mane.

Only the wicked king knew him. 'Ah, foundling!' he called scornfully, 'Have you found it more easy to promise than to fulfil?'

Then Perseus drew aside the goatskin and cried: 'Behold the Gorgon's head!'

And as the king and his guests looked at that dreadful face, they stiffened, each man where he sat, into a ring of cold grey stones.

And Perseus turned and left them.

But the king and his guests sat silently, with the winecups before them on the board, till the rafters crumbled above their heads, and the walls behind their backs, and the grass sprung up about their feet. And there they sit, a ring of grey stones, until this day.

Abridged and adapted by Eileen Colwell from
The Heroes by Charles Kingsley
(See Note, page 159)

The Dutch Cheese

Once upon a time there lived, with his sister Griselda, in a little
cottage near the Great Forest, a young farmer whose name was
John. Brother and sister, they lived alone, except for their sheep-
dog, Sly, their flock of sheep, the numberless birds of the forest,
and the 'fairies'. John loved his sister beyond telling; he loved
Sly; and he delighted to listen to the birds singing at twilight
round the darkening margin of the forest. But he feared and hated
the fairies. And, having a very stubborn heart, the more he
feared, the more he hated them; and the more he hated them, the
more they pestered him.

Now these were a tribe of fairies, sly, small, gay-hearted and
mischievous, and not of the race of fairies noble, silent, beautiful
and remote from man. They were a sort of gipsy-fairies, very
nimble and of aery and prankish company, and partly for
mischief and partly for love of her they were always trying to
charm John's dear sister Griselda away, with their music and
fruits and trickery. He more than half believed it was they who
years ago had decoyed into the forest not only his poor old father,
who had gone out faggot-cutting in his sheepskin hat with his ass,

but his mother too, who soon after, had gone out to look for him.

But fairies, even of this small tribe, hate no man. They mocked him and mischiefed him; they spilt his milk, rode astraddle on his rams; garlanded his old ewes with sow-thistle and briony, sprinkled water on his kindling wood, loosed his bucket into the well, and hid his great leather shoes. But all this they did, not for hate—for they came and went like evening moths about Griselda—but because in his fear and fury he shut up his sister from them, and because he was sullen and stupid. Yet he did nothing but fret himself. He set traps for them, and caught starlings; he fired his blunderbuss at them under the moon, and scared his sheep; he set dishes of sour milk in their way, and sticky leaves and brambles where their rings were green in the meadows; but all to no purpose. When at dusk, too, he heard their faint, elfin music, he would sit in the door blowing into his father's great bassoon till the black forest echoed with its sad, solemn, wooden voice. But that was of no help either. At last he grew so surly that he made Griselda utterly miserable. Her cheeks lost their scarlet and her eyes their sparkling. Then the fairies began to plague John in earnest—lest their lovely, loved child of man, Griselda, should die.

Now one summer's evening—and most nights are cold in the Great Forest—John, having put away his mournful bassoon and bolted the door, was squatting, moody and gloomy, with Griselda, on his hearth beside the fire. And he leaned back his great hairy head and stared straight up the chimney to where high in the heavens glittered a host of stars. And suddenly, while he lolled there on his stool moodily, watching them, there appeared against the dark sky a mischievous elvish head secretly peeping down at him; and busy fingers began sprinkling dew on his wide upturned face. He heard the laughter too of the fairies miching and gambolling on his thatch, and in a rage he started up, seized a round Dutch cheese that lay on a platter, and with all his force threw it clean and straight up the sooty chimney at the faces of mockery clustered above. And after that, though Griselda sighed at her spinning wheel, he heard no more. Even the cricket that had been whistling all through the evening, fell silent, and John supped on his black bread and onions alone.

Next day Griselda woke at dawn and put her head out of the little window beneath the thatch, and the day was white with mist.

'Twill be another hot day,' she said to herself, combing her beautiful hair.

But when John went down, so white and dense with mist were the fields, that even the green borders of the forest were invisible, and the whiteness went to the sky. Swathing and wreathing itself, opal and white as milk, all the morning the mist grew thicker and thicker about the little house. When John went out about nine o'clock to peer about him, nothing was to be seen at all. He could hear his sheep bleating, the kettle singing, Griselda sweeping, but straight up above him hung only, like a small round fruit, a little cheese-red beamless sun—straight up above him, though the hands of the clock were not yet come to ten. He clenched his fists and stamped in sheer rage. But no one answered him, no voice mocked him but his own. For when idle, mischievous fairies have played a trick on an enemy they soon weary of it.

All day long that little sullen lantern burned above the mist, sometimes red, so that the white mist was dyed to amber, and sometimes milky pale. The trees dropped water from every leaf. Every flower asleep in the garden was neckleted with beads; and nothing but an old drenched forest crow visited the lonely cottage that afternoon to cry, 'Kah, Kah, Kah!' and fly away.

But Griselda knew her brother's mood too well to speak of it or to complain. And she sang on gaily in the house, though she was more sorrowful than ever.

Next day John went out to tend his flocks. And wherever he went the red sun seemed to follow. When at last he found his sheep they were drenched with the clinging mist and were huddled together in dismay. And when they saw him it seemed that they cried out in one unanimous bleating voice: 'O ma-a-a-ster!'

And he stood counting them. And a little apart from the rest

53

stood his old ram Soll, with a face as black as soot; and there, perched on his back, impish and sharp and scarlet, rode and tossed and sang just such another fairy as had mocked John from the chimney-top. A fire seemed to break out in his body, and, picking up a handful of stones, he rushed at Soll through the flock. They scattered, bleating, out into the mist. And the fairy, all-acockahoop on the old ram's back, took its small ears between finger and thumb, and as fast as John ran, so fast jogged Soll, till all the young farmer's stones were thrown, and he found himself along in a quagmire so sticky and befogged that it took him till afternoon to grope his way out. And only Griselda's singing over her broth-pot guided him at last home.

Next day he sought his sheep far and wide, but not one could he find. To and fro he wandered, shouting and calling and whistling to Sly, till heartsick and thirsty, they were both wearied out. Yet bleatings seemed to fill the air, and a faint, beautiful bell tolled on out of the mist; and John knew the fairies had hidden his sheep and he hated them the more.

After that he went no more into the fields, brightly green beneath the enchanted mist. He sat and sulked, staring out of the door at the dim forests far away, glimmering faintly red beneath the small red sun. Griselda could not sing any more, she was too tired and hungry. And just before twilight she went out and gathered the last few pods of peas from the garden for their supper.

And while she was shelling them, John, within doors in the cottage, heard again the tiny timbrels and the distant horns, and the odd, clear, grasshopper voices calling and calling her, and he knew in his heart that, unless he relented and made friends with the fairies, Griselda would surely one day run away and leave him forlorn. He scratched his great head and gnawed his broad thumb. They had taken his father, they had taken his mother, they might take his sister—but he *wouldn't* give in.

So he shouted, and Griselda in fear and trembling came in out of the garden with her basket and basin and sat down in the gloaming to finish shelling her peas.

And as the shadows thickened and the stars began to shine, the malevolent singing came nearer, and presently there was a groping and stirring in the thatch, a tapping at the window, and John knew the fairies had come—not alone, not one or two or three, but in their company and bands—to plague him, and to entice away Griselda. He shut his mouth and stopped up his ears with his fingers, but when, with great staring eyes, he saw them capering like bubbles in a glass, like flames along straw, on his very doorstep, he could contain himself no longer. He caught up Griselda's bowl and flung it—peas, water and all—full in the snickering faces of the Little Folk! There came a shrill, faint twitter of laughter, a scampering of feet, and then all again was utterly still.

Griselda tried in vain to keep back her tears. She put her arms round John's neck and hid her face in his sleeve.

'Let me go!' she said, 'let me go, John, just a day and a night, and I'll come back to you. They are angry with us. But they love me; and if I sit on the hillside under the boughs of the trees beside the pool and listen to their music just a little while, they will make the sun shine again and drive back the flocks, and we shall be as happy as ever. Look at poor Sly, John dear, he is hungrier even than I am.' John heard only the mocking laughter and the tap-tapping and the rustling and the crying of the fairies, and he wouldn't let his sister go.

And it began to be marvellously dark and still in the cottage. No stars moved across the casement, no waterdrops glittered in the candleshine. John could hear only one low, faint, unceasing stir and rustling all around him. So utterly dark and still it was that even Sly woke from his hungry dreams and gazed up into his mistress's face and whined.

They went to bed; but still all night long while John lay tossing on his mattress, the rustling never ceased. The old kitchen clock ticked on and on, but there came no hint of dawn. All was pitch-black and now all was utterly silent. There wasn't a whisper, nor a creak, not a sigh of air, not a footfall of mouse, not a flutter of moth, not a settling of dust to be heard at all. Only desolate silence. And John at last could endure his fears and suspicions no longer. He got out of bed and stared from his square casement. He could see nothing. He tried to thrust it open; it would not move. He went downstairs and unbarred the door and looked out. He saw, as it were, a deep, clear, green shade, from behind which the songs of the birds rose faint as in a dream.

And then he sighed like a grampus and sat down, and knew that the fairies had beaten him. Like Jack's beanstalk, in one night had grown up a dense wall of peas. He pushed and pulled and hacked with his axe, and kicked with shoes, and buffeted with his blunderbuss. But it was all in vain. He sat down once more in his chair beside the hearth and covered his face with his hands. And at last Griselda, too, awoke, and came down with her candle. And she comforted her brother, and told him if he would do what she bade she would soon make all right again. And he promised her.

So with a scarf she bound tight his hands behind him; and with a rope she bound his feet together, so that he could neither run nor throw stones, peas or cheeses. She bound his eyes and ears and nose with a napkin, so that he could neither see, hear, smell, nor cry out. And, that done, she pushed and pulled him like a great bundle, and at last rolled him out of sight into the chimney-corner against the wall. Then she took a small sharp pair of needlework scissors that her godmother had given her, and snipped and snipped, till at last there came a little hole in the thick green hedge of peas. And, putting her mouth there she called softly through the little hole. And the fairies drew near the doorstep and nodded and listened.

And then and there Griselda made a bargain with them for the forgiveness of John—a lock of her golden hair; seven dishes of ewes' milk; three and thirty bunches of currants, red, white and black; a bag of thistledown; three handkerchiefs full of lambs' wool; nine jars of honey; a peppercorn of spice. All these (except the hair) John was to bring himself to their secret places as soon as he was able. Above all, the bargain between them was that Griselda would sit one full hour each evening of summer on the hillside in the shadow and greenness that slope down from the great forest towards the valley, where the fairies' mounds are, and where their tiny brindled cattle graze.

Her brother lay blind and deaf and dumb as a log of wood. She promised everything.

And then, instead of a rustling and a creeping, there came a rending and a crashing. Instead of green shade, light of amber; then white. And as the thick hedge withered and shrank, and the merry and furious dancing sun scorched and scorched and scorched, there came above the singing of the birds, the bleating of sheep—and behold sooty Soll and hungry Sly met square upon the doorstep; and all John's sheep shone white as hoarfrost in his pastures; and every lamb was garlanded with pimpernel and eyebright; and the old fat ewes stood still, with saddles of moss; and their laughing riders sat and saw Griselda standing at the doorway in her beautiful yellow hair.

As for John, tied up like a sack in the chimney-corner, down came his cheese again crash upon his head, and, not being able to say anything, he said nothing.

From *Collected Stories for Children* by
Walter de la Mare (Faber & Faber)
(See Note, page 160)

The Monster of Raasay

Long, long ago on the island of Raasay, close to Skye, there lived a man called McVurich, Lord of Raasay. He was a hard man and cruel and many were afraid of him.

One day he was out hunting. He had killed a deer and was about to carry it home when he heard a faint sound of distress from the heather-covered hillside. Searching among the heather, he discovered a tiny furry creature with bright frightened eyes. It seemed to be very young and it was shivering with cold.

The Lord of Raasay was seldom kind, but for once he felt sorry for the little creature and buttoned it inside his coat to warm it. Then he shouldered his deer and made his way home.

As he ate his supper he wondered what the small creature could be. It was not like any animal he knew and yet it was not human. As he sat thinking he was suddenly conscious that, although it was not yet sunset, the room was dark. The window was blocked by a huge head, a head so ugly and terrifying that it could only be that of the Raasay Monster, a beast that was neither dragon nor giant but still more dreadful. It was said that the Monster hated men and destroyed any that came in its path. Although McVurich was afraid of no one, his blood ran cold as he

58

looked at the Monster's face for the first time.

The Monster spoke in a harsh voice. 'I know well that you have found my child, McVurich,' it said. 'Give him back to me.'

'You can have him,' said the man boldly, 'if you pay me a proper ransom.'

'Give him back to me at once or I shall destroy your house and you,' threatened the Monster.

'If you destroy my house, you will kill your child also,' said the Lord of Raasay. 'I shall not let him go without a ransom.'

The Monster hesitated. 'What is your price?' it asked.

'You must build me a causeway across Loch Storab, so that I can bring my cattle home without danger.'

'That will be difficult!' said the Monster. 'Do you promise me faithfully that you will give me back my child if I do this?'

'You shall have him,' promised the Lord of Raasay.

At midnight the window was darkened again by the Monster's head. 'All is finished,' it said. 'Now give me back my child.'

'He is to be had for a ransom,' said McVurich once more.

'I have paid the ransom,' said the Monster angrily. 'Give me back my child!'

'First bring me home every peat I have on the hill and stack them all neatly at the house end,' demanded McVurich.

In vain the Monster stormed at him and threatened him. McVurich would not yield and the Monster was afraid its child might be harmed if it did not do what the cruel McVurich wanted. So once more the Monster went away and did as it was bid.

At dawn it returned, weary and angry. 'I have finished the task. Now give me back my child.'

'He is to be had for a ransom,' said McVurich for the third time.

'I have paid the ransom twice over. I will not pay again,' shouted the Monster hoarsely.

McVurich shook the small furry creature that was the Monster's child so that it wailed aloud. 'I will do one thing more and only one thing,' said the Monster hastily.

'You must build me a house larger and finer than all other houses on the island and thatch it with birds' feathers, no two

59

alike,' said the Lord of Raasay.

'That will be hard indeed,' said the Monster. 'You are a cruel man, McVurich. With every stone I use, there shall be bad luck, with every feather a curse.'

'I care not!' said McVurich carelessly. He gave the child a kick so that it cried out in protest.

'I will do what you ask,' said the Monster quickly. 'Only keep the child safe for me.'

The Monster built the house with such speed that it seemed that stones and wood flew into place on their own. Every tree willingly gave wood for the building, every stone yielded itself without complaint.

But how to thatch the house with feathers and no two alike? The Monster had no power over the birds of the air.

But even the birds, unlike McVurich, had pity for the Monster's plight. McVurich's house grew dark as night, so many were the flocks of birds flying wingtip to wingtip from the east and the west, from the north and the south. Each bird laid one feather on the roof of the new house. The last feather was placed as the cocks crew for dawn.

'Now give me back my child!' screamed the Monster in so terrible a voice that even McVurich shrank back in terror. The sun was blotted out by the vast flocks of birds that hovered overhead, the sound of their wings was like a mighty roaring wind. McVurich feared for his life if he did not keep his promise this time.

'Take your child,' he cried, 'and good riddance!' And he thrust the tiny furry creature out of the window.

The Monster caught up the child. Away it sped, whither no one knows, a canopy of birds flying overhead. Never again was the Monster seen on the Isle of Raasay, neither did McVurich see good luck again. And as for the wonderful house, a great gale carried it away until not one feather remained.

Adapted from a Scottish folktale by Eileen Colwell
(See Note, page 161)

The Little Brown Bees
of Ballyvourney

Once in the long ago there were no bees in all Ireland. Flowers there were a-plenty, starring the fields and hills and growing rank in the fen lands through the short months of summer.

And there were gardens hidden behind convent walls and tended lovingly, full of sweet herbs and old flowering shrubs and strange little-known blossoms. Ballyvourney had the loveliest garden of them all, and it was grown and tended by St Gobnat and her nuns, and was the joy and pride of their convent. It would have been a pleasant sight to see the white-robed sisters busy amongst the flowering herbs, weeding, culling, cherishing, their faces as fair as the blossoms beneath their busy fingers. Doubtless they chattered and laughed, maybe they hummed little lilting tunes as they worked, but save for the soft ripple of their voices, sudden bird song or swift whir of wings, there would be naught to hear. No drone and buzz of pilfering busy bee, warm and lulling to the ear, and an inseparable part of all thought and memory of gardens.

But in Wales there were bees enough and to spare, and especially at the monastic school of St David's which was called Menevia.

Indeed beehives were reckoned there as the richest possession of the monastery, and none of the brothers had a more important task to perform than Madomnoc, who was master of the bees.

Madomnoc was Irish, and sure one would know it by the way of him. Such gentleness of touch, such a rich softness of voice, such a knowledgeable eye, it would seem that the little creatures, being uncanny wise, knew that he loved them, and they prospered under his handling. Never was there such a golden-clear honey, never such hives, clean and busy and productive, never such swarms that gathered and rose in the air about each new queen, only to fall back again into the orchards of Menevia where Brother Madomnoc would set a fresh dwelling for them and tend and love them all, old and young, queen, worker, soldier, and drone. Already the fame of those little brown bees of Menevia had spread far and wide.

There came a day when Madomnoc had finished his studies and fulfilled his vows and done all that he felt the good God and St David required of him at Menevia. So he sought out and gained permission to return to his barren coast of Ireland, and was minded to go about among his native people sharing with them all the beautiful things he had learned of the Lord Christ and His kingdom. The people of Menevia were loath to bid him farewell, for they loved the Irish brother with his gentle humour and quiet ways and the roll and burr of his tongue that has ever warmed the cockles of the heart when an Irishman spoke, be it then or now. But at length, with his meagre possessions in a bundle on his back, with a staff in his hand, a smile on his lips, and tears in the blue eyes of him, Madomnoc waved a last goodbye to those upon the shore and sat him down in the boat that was to bear him across the Irish sea to his old home.

When they were well out of sight of land, the sailor folk suddenly became distraught and pointed and gesticulated so that captain and passengers wondered what the to-do was about.

And, behold! a brown cloud following after them like dust or smoke, albeit the breeze was languid, and off the starboard side of the vessel, so that there could be naught from the land blown upon it. By little and little the cloud gained upon them. Soon it was over and around them, and Madomnoc lifted up his arms and laughed a rich chuckling Irish laugh, for he saw and understood. The little brown bees, his bees from Menevia, had followed after him! They swarmed about him, they covered his hair and his face and hands, they droned and whirred and sang to him. All the other people upon the boat drew apart from him, astonished and fearful.

'Man, thou wilt be stung to death!' cried the captain.

'Ay, let us get a torch and smoke them away,' suggested a passenger.

'Nay, nay!' said Brother Madomnoc decidedly. 'By the faith of St Patrick, you will do no such thing! Ach, would you slay my children before the very eyes of me? My little brown bees! They will do no harm at all, at all; see you not? They love me!'

That was all very well said, but what was to do about it? The bees belonged to St David's School. The monks would be loath to lose the wealth of their honey, and how would Madomnoc fare if he went about the little Irish parishes with a great cloud of bees accompanying him and doubtless drowning out every sermon he preached with their noisy humming? There was naught for it but to turn back.

So Madomnoc returned to Menevia with his bees about him and saw to it that they were comfortably housed, then stole forth at night while they were all sleeping, thinking to befool the little creatures. But not they! Again they followed him, and he came back with them, and yet again; and then St David himself summoned the Irish Brother and bade him take the brown bees with him and keep them for himself, seeing they would in no wise remain behind without him.

Then he caused to be fashioned for them a strong brown hive, and he bade his bees enter it and be still, talking to them in the gentle, coaxing manner that was his wont, and they seemed to understand. Once more he set forth in a ship and, bearing his hive with him, crossed the sea without further incident and landed on the Irish shore.

He had heard the fame of St Gobnat and her convent garden, so lovely and old and full of fragrant bloom, and he thought no better home than that could be found for his little brown bees, so thither he took them. Very carefully he explained to the sisters how they should be tended and watched and loved, and on the bees themselves he laid a charge, firm and commanding though gently spoken. He had not thought before to speak to them directly. They must stay in the lovely garden of Ballyvourney, making the sound of it as sweet and fair as was the sight and the fragrance of it; they must be wise and industrious and share the golden-brown honey of their stores with those who provided for them; and above all, they must keep watch and ward over the kind nuns that nothing and no one harmful or ungentle should ever touch or molest them in any way. Then he folded his hands in his black sleeves, bowed his head, and went upon his way.

Time passed. The little brown bees were obedient to the voice they had loved, and they carried on their business in the hives as industriously and contentedly as ever they had done in the orchards of St David's. St Gobnat and the sisters tended them well, and the garden hummed and whirred, the blossoms bowed their lovely heads to the brown pilferers, and the sound in the rose bushes and trellises and multi-coloured flower beds was as warm and sweet as the fragrance thereof.

There came at last a day black and heavy with portent. The nuns gathered, trembling and whispering, about their sainted abbess, their tasks neglected, their busy fingers idle or nervously a-flutter, their faces as white as the wimples that covered their heads. Up from the village beyond the hill had run a messenger nigh dead with fear. Pirates, he said, fierce, wild men with blond hair and steel-blue eyes, tall and powerful, had landed from open vessels, and they were even then burning, pillaging, slaying. Ere long they would have worked their savage will upon the folk of the village and would be up and over the hill to desecrate the convent, steal its fabled gold, and mete out death to the white-robed sisters.

St Gobnat drew herself up, tall, commanding, unafraid.

'Come, my children,' said she, 'put away fear, and the blanched cheek and troubled eye of cowards. Are we not the brides of Heaven? Yes, and the guardians of our convent treasure. Let us do our part with confidence, and the Lord will send us succour in our hour of need.'

A murmur swelled; heads nodded to one another, and then lifted bravely as the lady abbess looked from face to face.

'And now come quickly,' she continued. 'Let us take the golden chalices and patens, the reliquaries, the cross and all the sacred altar furnishings, and hide them in the cave whereof you know. And let the precentress and those under her look well to the manuscripts and parchment rolls and secure them in the secret aumbry. And, Sister Sacristant, bear in all haste the bones and precious relics of our patron saint to the vault beneath the holy-water stoup. When all is done, gather with me in the garden, and we will watch and pray.'

Swiftly they scattered like a flock of white birds raised by the step of a hunter. This way and that they fluttered, and before long the sanctuary was bare of its treasure, the book shelves empty, the shrines open and gaping. Singly and in small groups, they gathered in the garden, and while the little brown bees hummed and droned about them, they knelt among the flowers in prayer.

Nor did they have long to wait. Harsh shouts, guttural cries, the clank of steel and tread of heavy boots broke the quiet of the garden, and in through the battered gates thundered the pirates, their eyes a-flame, their cruel faces eager and hideous.

St Gobnat rose from her knees and walked with slow fearless dignity to meet them.

'Tread not you the flowers of Ballyvourney,' said she, 'nor lay your impious hands on aught within these walls, for we and these and all herein are the Lord God's to do with as He wishes.'

The captain of the band flung her roughly aside. He understood no word of her language, and cared not. The men crowded after him, towering above the frightened women, thrusting this way and that.

'Gold!' said one, mouthing the only Gaelic word he could utter.

'Gold!' shouted another.

'Gold?' said St Gobnat, smiling grimly. 'Ay, we have gold, a liquid gold, purer and sweeter than any blood-stained pirate hand among you all has ever touched.'

She beckoned and they followed, crushing the flowers beneath their brutal feet. Under the low trees at the bottom of the garden stood the hives. St Gobnat led them hither.

'Come, little brown bees,' said she softly. 'Robbers would steal your gold. Come forth and protect it and us.'

Swiftly she turned over the hives, one by one, and out they came, clouds upon clouds of brown stinging fire. The sisters watched, aghast and then a-twitter with merriment. Not a single bee touched the Lady Gobnat or any whose white hands had tended them, but as an army furious for battle they attacked the men! They covered those brutish cruel faces, they swarmed over the hands, the bare, knotted knees; they crept beneath the clothing and buried their hot, tiny swords in the flesh of one and all, till the captain and every member of his band turned and fled, howling! Out through the garden gates they raced, down the long hill, through the smoking, ravaged village, to the boats beached in a long line upon the shore. With wild hands and stamping feet they plunged and stumbled, cursing and bellowing and roaring in pain and rage. Somehow the boats were thrust out upon the waves; in confusion and turmoil the pirates tumbled into them, bent to their oars, and sped out and away. The brown stinging cloud followed after them, mile upon mile, until they disappeared beyond the grey horizon.

That night Mother Gobnat and her nuns replaced the sacred furnishings upon the altar, tenderly refilled the shrines, laid the priceless vellum and parchment volumes again on the aumbry shelves and went about their way in confidence and joy. But not quite in their accustomed quietness; now and again there would be a twitter and a girlish giggle, and then a burst of laughter as one group after another brought to mind the uproarious retreat of the fierce Danish pirates who had been minded to pillage and destroy their defenceless convent and themselves.

And the little brown bees? They returned the very next day to the garden, and all Ballyvourney was sweet again with their busy and triumphant humming. The fame of them spread far and wide, and their children's children and all their progeny peopled the Irish land and have kept the faith, as Madomnoc bade them, from that day to this.

From *Told on the King's Highway* by Eleanore M. Jewett (Harrap)

(See Note, page 162)

Flannan Isle

Though three men dwell on Flannan Isle
To keep the lamp alight,
As we steered under the lee, we caught
No glimmer through the night.

A passing ship at dawn had brought
The news, and quickly we set sail
To find out what strange thing might ail
The keepers of the deep-sea light.

The winter day broke clear and bright,
With glancing sun and glancing spray,
While o'er the swell our boat made way,
As gallant as a gull in flight.

But as we neared the lonely Isle
And looked up at the naked height,
And saw the lighthouse towering white
With blinded lantern, that all night
Had never shot a spark
Of comfort through the dark,

So ghostly in the cold sunlight
It seemed, that we were struck the while
With wonder all too dread for words.
And as into the tiny creek
We stole, beneath the hanging crag
We saw three queer, black, ugly birds—
Too big, by far, in my belief
For cormorant or shag—
Like seamen sitting bolt-upright
Upon a half-tide reef:
But as we neared they plunged from sight
Without a sound or spurt of white.

And still too mazed to speak,
We landed and made fast the boat
And climbed the track in single file,
Each wishing he were safe afloat,
On any sea, however far,
So be it far from Flannan Isle:
And still we seemed to climb and climb
As though we'd lost all count of time
And so must climb for evermore;
Yet, all too soon, we reached the door—
The black sun-blistered lighthouse door,
That gaped for us ajar.

As on the threshold for a spell
We paused, we seemed to breathe the smell
Of limewash and of tar,
Familiar as our daily breath,
As though 'twere some strange scent of death;
And so yet wondering side by side
We stood a moment, still tongue-tied,
And each with black foreboding eyed
The door ere we should fling it wide
To leave the sunlight for the gloom:

Till, plucking courage up, at last
Hard on each other's heels we passed,
Into the living-room.

Yet, as we crowded through the door
We only saw a table spread
For dinner, meat and cheese and bread,
But all untouched and no one there;
As though when they sat down to eat,
Ere they could even taste,
Alarm had come and they in haste
Had risen and left the bread and meat,
For at the table-head a chair
Lay tumbled on the floor.

We listened, but we only heard
The feeble chirping of a bird
That starved upon its perch;
And, listening still, without a word
We set about our hopeless search.
We hunted high, we hunted low,
And soon ransacked the empty house;
Then o'er the Island, to and fro
We ranged, to listen and to look
In every cranny, cleft or nook
That might have hid a bird or mouse:
But though we searched from shore to shore
We found no sign in any place,
And soon again stood face to face
Before the gaping door,
And stole into the room once more
As frightened children steal.
Ay, though we hunted high and low
And hunted everywhere,
Of the three men's fate we found no trace
Of any kind in any place

But a door ajar, and an untouched meal,
And an overtoppled chair.

And as we listened in the gloom
Of that forsaken living-room—
A chill clutch on our breath—
We thought how ill-chance came to all
Who kept the Flannan Light,
And how the rock had been the death
Of many a likely lad—
How six had come to a sudden end
And three had gone stark mad,
And one, whom we'd all known as friend,
Had leapt from the lantern one still night
And fallen dead by the lighthouse wall—
And long we thought
On the three we sought,
And of what might yet befall.

Like curs a glance has brought to heel
We listened, flinching there,
And looked and looked on the untouched meal
And the overtoppled chair.

We seemed to stand for an endless while,
Though still no word was said,
Three men alive on Flannan Isle
Who thought on three men dead.

From *Collected Poems* by Wilfrid Gibson
(Macmillan)
(See Note, page 162)

The Little Wee Tyke
A Story from Northumberland

There was a little wee tyke and he was black, so nobody wanted him.

He wasn't so big as the house-cat, so nobody wanted him for a house-dog either.

They said he was no use at all and they were going to drown him when a poor, ragged little lassie begged for him and got him.

She ran home with him. 'Mammy! I've brought a little wee tyke!' she cried.

'There's no water for the porridge,' said her mother. 'The well's bewitched. He'll die of thirst like us all.'

'Not if I'm about,' said the little wee tyke. 'Let me alone to deal with this.'

Then the farmer came in.

'I can't get out to my sheep,' he said. 'The gate's bewitched and the ewes and the lambs need watching against hill foxes.'

'Not if I'm about,' said the little wee tyke. 'Leave me alone to deal with them.'

Then the son came in.

'The cow's bewitched. There's not a drop of milk to sell.'

Then his little boy came in.

'The hens are bewitched. There's no eggs and they'll never cackle or walk about any more.'

'Not if I'm about,' said the little wee tyke. 'Let me alone to deal with this.'

'You!' they all cried out angrily. 'Get out!' They started to throw things at him. The little lassie picked him up. 'You!' said the little wee lassie. 'Could you? Would you?'

'I would and what's more I will,' said the little wee tyke and out of the door he went.

'He can't get out any more than we can,' said the farmer. But he had.

'You can't pass through,' said the gate. 'Old Witch Nanny laid it on me to keep back all who belong here.'

'I don't belong here *yet*,' said the little wee tyke and he went through to the sheep. After he had rounded them up so nicely and quietly into the fold by the wall he went back to the hen-house and carried the twelve hens safe inside. 'I don't belong here *yet* so I'll break the mischief on you. When I've fetched your water, you can each lay an egg for me.'

Then he went down to the well and the family were all watching by now. He scratched all round where the spring ran out. 'Old Witch Nanny laid it on me not to run freely for any who belong here,' said the well. 'I don't belong here *yet*,' said the little wee tyke and he kicked away the witchstone and the water ran all down by the door and the mother got a pailful for the porridge.

Then the farmer went out to the fold and the little boy ran and found twelve eggs and the cow was milked.

'You all said we needed a dog,' said the little lassie.

'I've not done yet,' said the little wee tyke.

73

But they all came running back and crying, 'The witch is on her way here!' and ran to bolt the door, but the little wee tyke said , 'Let me out first. I'll deal with her,' and they shut him out and the little lassie cried.

Old Witch Nanny walked widdershins all round the farm. 'That'll hold them fast,' she cackled.

'Oh no, it won't. Not a bit,' barked the little wee tyke, 'because I've come behind you backwards and scratched your footprints all out.'

Old Witch Nanny turned around in terror and dropped her broom. 'That's clever, that is,' said the little wee tyke, and stood *across* [crosswise] it and then all she dare do was to shriek 'Scat!' at him.

'I'm not a house-cat,' said the little wee tyke. 'I can use my teeth as well as bark.'

Then Old Nanny the Witch tried to climb up the thatch-roof but the little wee tyke took a good bite of her left leg and hung on as she climbed. When he let go and rolled down to the ground, she sat on the roof bleeding and yelling and could never do any mischief any more. Then she fell off the roof and lay in the farmyard. 'I'm dying!' she whimpered.

'Not just yet,' said the little wee tyke. 'Old Nick has got to fetch you and we don't want him here—and he doesn't like the look of me and my teeth. Take yourself away and die Somewhere Else before he takes you there!'

Away she hobbled and crawled right out of sight. And there was thunder and lightning and a great green flame.

Then the little lass called the little wee tyke to come in.

'I don't belong,' said the little wee tyke.

'We all want you,' said the little boy.

'But I'm black, ' said the little wee tyke.

'So is our house-cat,' said the mother, 'and she is almost as good and clever as you.'

'I'm too small,' said the little wee tyke.

'You got good teeth,' said the father.

'You won't chase me with the poker or throw things at me, or tread on me when I'm sleeping?'

'Never!' they cried, and the little lassie brought him a bowl of milk.

And when he had lapped it all up he came in. 'This is about my size,' he said and went to sleep in one of the farmer's slippers.

From *Forgotten Folktales of the English Counties* collected by Ruth Tongue (Routledge & Kegan Paul)
(See Note, page 163)

Sohrab and Rustem

One day the Persian hero, Rustem, riding his horse Rakush, was hunting a lion. Weary with the chase, he lay down to rest under a tree. When he awoke his horse had disappeared. Rakush had been stolen by thieves.

Rustem was dismayed for he loved Rakush dearly. He was angry also that anyone should dare to rob him, he the great Rustem.

He followed Rakush's tracks immediately to the gate of a city several miles into enemy country. There he demanded to see the ruler of the city. No one dared to oppose him and the ruler promised to punish the thieves himself as soon as they could be found. To placate Rustem he invited him to a feast and when he found that Rustem had fallen in love with his beautiful daughter, Taminah, he offered Rustem her hand in marriage. Rakush too was found and restored to him.

But Rustem could stay only a short time with his bride, then he had to return to his own country. Before leaving Taminah, he took

76

a jewelled amulet from his arm and gave it to her. 'Perhaps the gods will send us a child,' he said. 'If it is a girl, bind this amulet in her hair; if it is a boy, bid him wear it on his arm as I do.'

Rustem rode away and told no one of his marriage, for he knew that the Persian emperor wished him to marry a maiden of his own country.

In due course a son was born to Taminah and because he laughed and smiled so merrily, she named him Sohrab, the Child of Smiles. She sent the news of the birth to Rustem but told him that the baby was a girl, for she feared that Rustem would take the child away if he knew that it was a son. Rustem sent rich gifts of rubies and sacks of gold to his daughter—and forgot her.

Sohrab grew quickly. He was no ordinary child, for at nine years of age he was as skilful in riding and fighting as most grown men. He was handsome and gay and outdid all his companions in sports.

One day he came to his mother and asked, 'Who is my father, mother? I am ashamed that I do not know.'

'You need never be ashamed of your father, my son, for he is Rustem, the Persian hero,' answered his mother.

'Rustem is my father!' exclaimed Sohrab. 'I must tell everyone!' and he was about to rush away when his mother caught him by the arm and begged him to be silent.

'Do not be so hasty, my son,' she said. 'Your father is a Persian and an enemy of this country and of all Tartars. If the King of the Tartars should hear that Rustem has a son, he will kill you.'

'Then I will seek out my father secretly and tell him he has a son,' said Sohrab eagerly.

'Do not leave me so soon!' begged his mother. 'When you are older you may go with my blessing.'

So Sohrab stayed with her for a time, but at last he could delay no longer so eager was he to find his father. He bade farewell to his mother and rode away on his black horse, attended by only a few companions of his own age. The little band was soon known far and wide, for Sohrab's courage and skill in arms gave them the victory against the enemy wherever they went.

When the King of the Tartars heard of Sohrab and his band, he knew that this was no ordinary young warrior and he soon guessed that only Rustem could be the father of such a son. He determined that Sohrab should meet Rustem in battle—without knowing whom he was fighting—and that when he had killed Rustem, Sohrab himself should die. Thus the two men who might conquer the Tartars would no longer be a danger. But Rustem must not know that he had a son; Sohrab must not be allowed to recognise his father.

So the King of the Tartars suggested cunningly that he would give Sohrab an army to lead against the Persians. Once the Emperor of the Persians was conquered, then Rustem should be made emperor in his place. Sohrab, being young and impetuous, believed that this could happen and was glad for his father's sake. Riding at the head of an army, he set out to invade Persia.

In Persia the emperor heard of the invasion and of the brave young leader. He summoned Rustem to him and said: 'I am told that the Tartars are led by a young warrior who is your equal in skill and strength. It is my will that you ride out against him and kill him.'

At once Rustem mounted his horse and rode off to battle. He would soon get rid of this conceited young man, he thought, and return home. No man could hope to oppose Rustem with his lifetime of experience of battle, least of all a young man.

Rustem mingled with the Persian host and watched the Tartar camp. He soon picked out a tall young man on a black horse who was always in the thick of the battle. He was certainly brave and strong—unusually strong. 'Ah,' sighed Rustem, 'would that I had a son like this young man! This must be the Sohrab of whom they speak.'

In the Tartar camp, Sohrab watched for Rustem in the Persian host. He saw a tall warrior, head and shoulders above any other, riding a golden yellow horse. Wherever he rode the Tartars fell back before him. Surely this must be Rustem!

'Is not that the mighty Rustem?' he asked the soldiers. But they had been warned on no account to tell Sohrab what he wanted to know, so they replied, 'We do not know . . .'

Sohrab was determined to force a meeting between Rustem and himself, so next day he rode boldly into the open sandy space between the two armies and shouted, 'I challenge your mightiest warrior to fight me in single combat!'

But no man dared meet Sohrab, so great was his fame.

At last Rustem himself rode forth. 'Shame upon you, Persians!' he cried. 'This is only a stripling. I will fight him myself.' He rode forward but he left his shield with its distinctive device behind and took that of another warrior, for he felt it beneath his pride to fight so young a man.

But Sohrab watching eagerly saw how strong and proud was this man and cried, 'Surely you are Rustem?'

'Rustem! Would the mighty Rustem fight against a young dog such as you?' said Rustem scornfully. 'Fight for your life, young man. Soon your bones will strew the sand.'

'I am no girl to turn pale with fear,' said Sohrab angrily. 'If you were indeed Rustem, I would never fight you, but you are not Rustem, so I fear you not.'

The two warriors rode against each other fiercely and the battle began. Both armies drew back to watch while the two champions fought, as was the custom. All day the battle swung to and fro, but neither champion could gain the advantage, so evenly were they matched.

As evening drew on and darkness came, Rustem said, 'Let us rest. We are both weary—but we will fight again tomorrow.'

And so ended the first day.

On the second day, the two champions took bow and arrows and shot against each other. When all their arrows were spent, they dismounted and wrestled, gasping and straining. Rustem was amazed at Sohrab's strength and skill. At one moment, he even had Rustem at his mercy, but a strange uneasiness kept Sohrab from delivering the death blow.

So ended the second day.

That night the Tartars reproached Sohrab for sparing Rustem's life.

'Are you sure that this mighty man is not Rustem?' asked Sohrab. 'God forbid that I should kill my own father!'

'This man is *like* Rustem, it is true,' answered the soldiers, 'but he is not Rustem.'

'Then tomorrow the battle shall be ended,' promised Sohrab. 'One of us shall die.'

And in the Persian camp, Rustem, too, determined that the third day of the battle should be decisive. He was ashamed that Sohrab had had him at his mercy and yet had spared his life. He, the great Rustem, to be bested by a boy! Tomorrow he must kill Sohrab.

Thus dawned the third day of the fight. Each army drew back again and into the sandy space, now red with blood, rode the two champions, Rustem with his massive helmet from which waved a scarlet plume, Sohrab with his helmet decorated with shining silver. Each bore a long lance with a coloured pennon; each rode a magnificent horse.

Rustem's heart was heavy in spite of his pride and anger. He was strangely reluctant to kill this young man. Sohrab, too, was uneasy. Even now he halted and said, 'Let us make peace and exchange gifts, brave warrior. We have fought well and honourably. It is enough.'

But Rustem said harshly, 'We are enemies and must remain so. Guard yourself, bold youth. Today you die!'

Lances couched, they rode at each other again and met with such a shock that the earth itself trembled. At that moment the sun was blotted out and a chill wind wailed across the sand.

First Rustem gained the advantage, then Sohrab. Then each man dismounted and bade his horse stand aside. Men marvelled to see how ferociously they fought. To and fro they staggered, locked in combat, until Rustem, hard pressed, shouted—without knowing it—his battle cry, *'Rustem!'*

At the sound of that name, Sohrab, about to strike, stood dismayed and defenceless. His shield dropped from his nerveless hand and Rustem pierced him to the heart.

Mortally wounded, Sohrab fell to the ground, but yet he

gasped, 'You may kill me, but you will never escape the vengeance of my father, the mighty Rustem.'

'Your father!' said Rustem. 'Rustem has no son, boy, he has only a daughter.'

'He *has* a son,' gasped Sohrab, 'and I am he. Alas, I shall never meet my father now.' He closed his eyes wearily, then said painfully, 'The amulet on my arm—Rustem's—take it, stranger—give it to my mother, Taminah—I implore you . . .'

And Rustem, lifting Sohrab's arm, saw his amulet, the amulet he had given to his wife so long ago for their child.

'Alas,' he said brokenly. 'I am your father. I am Rustem himself—and I have killed my own son!' Tenderly he lifted the dying Sohrab in his arms, while Rakush came closer with drooping head and mane sweeping the sand, to stand by his master's side.

'Rakush—is it Rakush?' murmured Sohrab, and lifted his hand feebly to stroke the silky neck.

Then Rustem, the fierce and merciless warrior, wept and cried, 'Would I might die in your place, my son. I am weary of this life of blood and battle . . .'

'Grieve not for me,' whispered Sohrab. 'Death comes to all,' and even as he spoke, he fell back lifeless. Thus came Death to him.

'So, on the bloody sand, Sohrab lay dead;
And the great Rustem drew his horseman's cloak
Down o'er his face, and sate by his dead son . . .
And night came down over the solemn waste,
And the two gazing hosts, and that sole pair . . .
And Rustem and his son were left alone.'

Traditional. Adapted by Eileen Colwell.
(See Note, page 164)

The Dog

Once upon a time there was a dog who was very fond of sausages.
His name was Sheltie.

His mother said: 'If you want some sausages you must go and
earn some money to pay for them.'

So Sheltie licked his mother goodbye, and went out into the
world to seek his fortune.

He went down Highgate Hill and met a cat that was made of
stone, and it said to him, 'Why don't you go and see the Lord
Mayor? He wants some dogs to wag their tails when they see the
Lord Mayor's Show.'

'All, right!' said Sheltie, and he went and saw the Lord Mayor,
who said: 'I'll give you half a sausage if you come and wag your
tail.'

Sheltie felt so sad at getting offered only half a sausage that he
put his tail between his legs.

The Lord Mayor was angry. 'If that's how you wag your tail,'
he said, 'you shan't have anything.'

So Sheltie said goodbye to him and went away.

Just then the Head Postman of London was passing and said, 'You can come and work in the Post Office and lick stamps for people.'

So Sheltie went there and licked stamps for people so that they could stick them on the envelopes; and the postman gave him some sausages.

One day Sheltie had a pain in his tummy, so the postman took him to the vet.

The vet shone a torch in Sheltie's mouth and said, 'Why, he's swallowed lots of stamps and that's what's given him a pain. And look,' he added, 'there's a stamp sticking to his back too.'

And so there was!

'Oh, well,' said the postman. 'If he's got a stamp on him he ought to be posted.' So he took Sheltie to the Post Office and said goodbye to him and gave him to the man at the parcels counter. But because he hadn't got any address on him he was sent to the Lost Property Office.

Sheltie didn't like it very much there. But he met a horse. It was a lost parcel too, and was wrapped in brown paper, though its head was sticking out.

'I've got an Aunt who lives in the country,' said the horse. 'She belongs to a man who has sausages for tea every Saturday.'

'Oh, sausages, sausages, sausages!' said Sheltie.

'Would you like to come and live with my Aunt?' said the horse.

'Oh, *yes!*' said Sheltie.

So they ran away and stayed with the man and the horse's aunt.

And from that day onwards, Sheltie guarded the man's house and was given delicious sausages for his supper every Saturday.

From *The Adventures of Mandy Duck* by Donald Bisset
(Methuen Children's Books)
(See Note, page 165)

Golden Hair

Once upon a time there was a young peasant maiden who had beautiful long golden hair. And the wicked Count Rinaldo fell in love with that golden hair and said he would take the maiden for his bride.

'Ah!' said Golden Hair's mother. 'Now our little daughter will be a countess. How fine that is!'

'Oh ho!' said Golden Hair's father. 'Count Rinaldo shall have her, yes, he shall have her; but he shall pay me a bag of gold.'

But Golden Hair loved a peasant lad called Pietro. She would have nothing to do with the wicked Count.

Her mother wept and scolded, her father cursed and raged, and the wicked Count said, 'Bah! I will soon remove that worm out of my path!'

So the Count lay in wait for Pietro on a dark night, thinking to kill him. But when the Count fell on Pietro with his sword, Pietro drew his hunting knife to defend himself; and it wasn't Pietro who was killed in that struggle, but the Count.

Then Pietro fled to a far country, for the Count's people were after him to kill him. But before he went he managed to see Golden Hair and he said to her, 'Do not despair, my beloved! Wait for me, though it be one year, or two, or three. I will work hard and make a home for you. And one night I will come to fetch you and take you to our home.'

'I will wait,' said Golden Hair.

And she waited. One year passed, two years passed, three years passed. And after the three years, one day as Golden Hair was walking through the market, there came a little lad who thrust a letter into her hand and disappeared among the crowd.

The letter said, 'Our home is ready, Golden Hair. Look for me tonight between midnight and cockcrow. Look for me on a grey horse in the street outside your window.'

That night Golden Hair sat at her window, watching and waiting. She heard the church clock strike midnight—and surely she heard something else? Yes, the muffled steps of a horse down there in the street. And yes, the merest whisper of a voice: 'Golden Hair, Golden Hair, come down and go with me!'

'I come, I come, Pietro! Ah, how long I have waited!'

'Quick, quick, I have come to fetch you to our home.'

Golden Hair crept downstairs, opened the house door quietly—oh, how quietly—and stepped out into the night: all silent, all dark, the moon hidden behind a black cloud; the glimmer of a grey horse, the dusky shape of a rider muffled in a cloak, the whisper of a voice: 'Quick, quick, up behind me, Golden Hair!'

The rider reached down a hand. Golden Hair grasped it and sprang up behind him. In a moment they were off: *patata, patata, patata,* the horse going like the wind.

On, on, on, Golden Hair with her arms clasped round the body of the cloaked rider; on, on, on, clouds racing over the sky, the moon shining out bright and clear between them; on, on, on, *patata, patata, patata, faster, faster, faster, and faster*—on into a country Golden Hair had never seen before.

See, now they were passing a churchyard, the white gravestones gleaming in the moonlight; and hark, a loud voice calling from among the graves, 'The clouds part, the light of the moon shines clear like day. A youth rides with his maiden. Living maiden, are you not afraid?'

And Golden Hair called back, 'What should I fear when I have plighted my troth?'

On, on, on, *patata, patata, patata, go faster, go faster, go faster!* The world flying away under the horse's hoofs. See, now they were passing another churchyard, and again a loud voice called from among the graves, 'The moon shines bright as day. A youth rides with his maiden. Living maiden, are you not afraid to ride with the dead?'

And Golden Hair called back. 'What should I fear? I do not ride with the dead, I ride with my lover.'

'Ha! ha! ha! Ha! ha! ha!' Up from the graveyard rose shouts of laughter, and from the cloaked rider came a laugh louder than all the rest. 'Truly you ride with your lover, but truly you ride with the dead!'

The rider flung his cloak from his head and turned, and leered at Golden Hair.

And it was not Pietro. It was the ghost of Count Rinaldo.

'In hell I have burned, in hell I have waited,' screamed the ghost. 'In life you escaped me; in death you are mine!'

'Help, help, help!' Golden Hair slid from the horse, but the ghost seized her by her long hair.

'Help! Help! Help!' Was there no help for Golden Hair whirled along by the hair of her head by the side of the galloping horse? *Patata, patata, patata, go faster, go faster, go faster!* Towns, plains and mountains rushing to meet them, vanishing behind them, and there, at the world's end, the iron gates of the City of the Dead drawing nearer and nearer.

'Pietro! Pietro! Help! Pietro! Pietro! Pietro! Help! Help!'

And far away, Pietro riding through the night towards Golden Hair's village, heard that cry, swung round his horse, and galloped in pursuit.

86

'Golden Hair, Golden Hair, I am coming, my beloved, I am coming!'

Patata, patata, patata, go faster, go faster, go faster! Two riders, two grey horses galloping through the night towards the ends of the earth; see, the glow of a great fire over there beyond the ends of the earth, and rising dark and huge against the glow of that fire, the iron gates of the City of the Dead. And see, ahead of Pietro, a glitter of golden hair swinging wildly from the saddle of a galloping horse.

'Pietro! Pietro!'

Patata, patata, patata, go faster, go faster, go faster!

The moon shone clear from a black cloud. Pietro lashing his willing horse, was galloping nearer, ever nearer to the ghostly rider on the ghostly horse. But the huge iron gates of the City of the Dead were also drawing nearer, and those iron gates were slowly opening.

But Pietro was now abreast of the ghostly rider, and Pietro leaned from the saddle, drew his hunting knife, slashed through the golden hair clutched in the ghost's hand, snatched up his beloved and set her on his own horse, just as the iron gates of the City of the Dead swung wide open and the ghost, still clutching the golden hair, galloped through.

The iron gates shut with a clang behind the ghostly horse and the ghostly rider. Yes, Count Rinaldo had the golden hair, but he had nothing else. And since it was the golden hair that Count Rinaldo fell in love with, why then—let him be satisfied!

But Pietro carried Golden Hair away to his home in a far country, and there they married, and lived in peace and happiness ever after.

From *A Book of Ghosts and Goblins* by Ruth Manning-Sanders
(Methuen Children's Books)
(See Note, page 166)

Little Holger and His Flute

Every day Holger the shepherd boy sits on the gate, playing his pipe. Brown bare legs, a pair of tattered trousers, an old hat of his father's on his dark curly hair. Around him lie the flowering Alpine meadows, the mountains covered with perpetual snow. Holger is King of the World! After all, the cows follow him obediently when he leads them back to the cowshed each evening. And Lisa, too, lying asleep in the grass, acknowledges him as her master.

King of the World! When he plays his pipe the rabbits come frisking, their ears pricked so that they can hear better. The birds perch on the gate, flipping their tails to keep their balance. Holger is the first to be greeted by the morning sun when she peeps between the mountains; only then does she send her golden light down into the valley where the big people live.

Yes, little Holger is so powerful that once he even sent the devil about his business!

For a long time the devil had been plaguing the people below in the village. He whispered in the ear of Krol, a rich miserly farmer, that Hannes, the old and faithful servant who had worked for his father, was a thief. Krol chased Hannes angrily from the farm, telling him to starve for all he cared.

When drunken Geert came out of the tavern with his friend Klaas Bierpot, the devil stuck his hoof between their legs so that Geert landed on the hard cobblestones. With a diabolical laugh the devil sprang up into the tower, clasped the weathercock with his bony hands and swung round and round with pleasure. Geert thought that Klaas had tripped him up and was now laughing at him into the bargain, so he gave him a black eye.

One night, in the inn The Lion of Persia, the devil mixed up the shoes that had been left outside the bedroom doors to be cleaned so that, the next morning, a real battle broke out among the Alpine tourists!

Nothing was too much trouble for the devil when it came to tormenting the villagers. He mislaid collar studs, stopped clocks, mixed a sleeping draught in the night-watchman's coffee and, once, disguised as a nun, he even summoned the priest from his bed in the middle of the night with the message that Klaas Bierpot had expressed a need for the Last Rites—when, all the time, Klaas lay alone in the gutter in a drunken stupor.

Something had to be done! One Sunday morning the priest set out to banish the devil from the village. He himself walked at the front, chanting loudly; altar boys followed, swinging censers back and forth; then came the elders of the church and the other male citizens with lighted candles in their hands and, right at the back, the women followed, dressed in black and clutching their rosaries. Wolter and Jan Hendrik, the village policemen, walked alongside the procession with drawn swords; young farmers from surrounding districts had also volunteered to help protect the crowd; they were armed with whips and cudgels.

Everyone was convinced that the devil would take to his heels with all due speed when he saw this, but something else happened. From the tree in which he was hidden, the devil threw a purse full of gold pieces into the middle of the procession. He could afford to do this, of course, because he had mastered the art of making gold. But the worthy villagers beneath had not discovered this art, and it is not surprising that they all wanted the purse for themselves. Those who were walking at the front of the procession said that the purse was theirs, and those at the back rushed forward to claim the purse for themselves. The procession broke up in a confusion of quarrelling and fighting. The young farmers struck out with their cudgels and whips, the altar boys with their censers, and, in the excitement, Jan Hendrik nearly stabbed the priest in the paunch with his sword.

The devil sat sniggering in the tree, hugging himself with enjoyment. When he had seen enough, he sprang on to the back of a passing crow and disappeared. And those villagers who, after pushing, biting and scratching, managed to get hold of a gold piece, suddenly found that it had changed in their hand to a button—the very same button that they had put in the poor-box at mass the previous Sunday!

Everyone realised then that the devil had played a trick on them, and ashamed and dejected, they set off home to nurse their scratches and wounds.

No, it was not as easy as that to get rid of the devil. Not so long as he lived in their innermost hearts . . .

Only Holger, up there in the mountains, had escaped the torments of the devil. But then he was such a little fellow—he was easily overlooked!

So there he sat on the gate and played his flute in the warm morning sun; high in the sky a rising skylark echoed his happiness. Lisa gathered a garland of snapdragons, daisies, cuckoo-flowers and forget-me-nots, and now and then chased the butterflies that fluttered round her.

The devil pricked up his ears when he heard the cheerful sound of a shepherd's pipe in the distance, and crept nearer out of curiosity. 'Wait!' he thought, 'we don't yet have a flute player in hell. It would be a small catch but a charming one; the witches will have a merry tune for their dances. Yes, I'll give a ball down there in the flames. The boy's playing is not without merit, it gives me pleasure to hear him.'

And full of confidence—for he did not expect to have much trouble with this stupid little shepherd boy—he limped up the Alpine meadows where the brown mountain cows grazed to the sound of Holger's flute and the many-voiced ding-dong of the bells round their necks. With his most amiable grin, he walked up to Holger, who took the flute from his lips in astonishment.

'Your playing is not unpleasant,' said the devil. 'Where did you learn?'

Holger was not used to compliments. He played as well as he could and that was good enough for him. He looked down at his flute in embarrassment and asked: 'Who are you? Are you a tourist?'

'You've guessed!' said the devil. 'I've come to the mountains for health reasons.'

Holger could believe this. The strange gentleman looked awfully pale; the fresh mountain air would do him good.

'Yes, I'm a tourist, I enjoy travelling,' the devil went on. 'There are few places I haven't seen. Wouldn't you like to see something of the world as well? You only need to come along with me.'

Holger considered this. Lisa looked rather anxiously up at him.

'But what about my cows?' he asked.

The devil shrugged his shoulders contemptuously. 'There are cows everywhere.'

'That is true,' admitted Holger.

But just at that moment Bertha, the oldest cow, who had known him since his first day as a shepherd, came up and tried to lick him on the cheek. Holger scratched soft-eyed Bertha on the head and thought no more of foreign travel.

The devil meanwhile was thinking hard of ways of arousing the interest of this contented little fellow. Wait!

'May I have a look at your flute?' he asked.

Holger gave it to him. 'It's nothing special,' he said. 'I carved it myself.'

'May I try it?'

'Why not?'

The devil put the mouthpiece to his lips, but no sound came.

'Well, you have to learn how to play it, but after that it's easy,' said Holger. 'Look, this is what you should do.'

He played a long trill on the flute and a thrush somewhere among the fir trees gave answer.

'Beautiful,' said the devil. 'But you can only play a few notes on an ordinary wooden shepherd's pipe like this.'

'I don't mind. I don't know any others,' said Holger.

The devil winked. 'Wait a moment then.' He reached into his pocket and drew out a beautiful golden flute that sparkled in the sunlight.

'What on earth . . . ?' said Holger, startled. 'Where did you get that?'

'Just look at it very carefully,' said the devil.

Holger took the flute with timid respect. 'Is it really gold?'

'What do you think?'

The gentleman must be very rich, Holger thought, and asked: 'Will you play it?'

'Try it yourself.'

'I don't know if I can. Where are the little holes?'

'They're under the keys. This is no ordinary flute! You have to press the keys.'

'Here goes then.'

Holger tried to make a sound but without success. 'It's devilish difficult,' he sighed after he had tried several times.

'Oh, you'll learn soon enough. And then you won't believe your ears! You'll be able to play any tune you like on this golden flute.'

'Will you play it just once?

The devil took the flute from him, made sure that the keys were working properly, and then played a few swift notes, first in a low key and then in a high key. He knew that he could play well, and he looked expectantly at Holger. 'Now, what did you think of that?'

'Very fast, but it was also a little out of tune,' said Holger.

'What do you mean?'

'My ears hurt when it went so very high, really they did!'

'*I* thought it sounded horrible,' said Lisa, 'and look over there.'

A few rabbits and squirrels who had come to listen were now bounding rapidly away, and there was no sign of any birds in the trees at the edge of the meadow.

'Those stupid animals don't know good music when they hear it,' grumbled the devil crossly.

'But when Holger plays his flute, they all sit and listen quietly,' said Lisa.

The devil laughed mockingly. 'You're surely not trying to tell me that an ordinary shepherd's pipe sounds more beautiful than my golden flute?'

'*I* think so,' said Lisa.

'But what if I were to give you this golden flute as a present? Well, on one small condition . . .' The devil held the flute temptingly in front of him and Holger looked reluctantly at it again. The flute was so beautiful!

'Don't take it, Holger!' Lisa pleaded. 'What is the use of a golden flute if all the animals run away when you play it and it gives you a pain in the ears?'

'That's true,' Holger was forced to admit. 'It's certainly very beautiful to look at but will it still sound out of tune?'

The devil could hardly conceal his anger as he made the flute disappear again in his pocket.

'Why don't you go away? We were having such a pleasant time together,' said Lisa.

The devil made an impatient gesture. 'Mind your own business. I came here to grant Holger a wish as a tribute to his flute playing. If he doesn't want the golden flute, then perhaps he would like something else?'

Holger had begun to play his pipe again. As he played he looked towards the edge of the wood to see if the rabbits would return. And yes, a few twitching noses and pricked-up ears were peeping from the greenery again; the birds too were listening once more.

'You can see for yourself now,' said Holger.

The devil had to admit defeat. 'Yes, I can see,' he sighed. 'But before I go let me give you something all the same. I ask nothing in return, there are no conditions. Do you really wish for nothing in the world?'

Holger thought for a moment. 'Perhaps,' he hesitated, 'but you could not grant it.'

The devil laughed slyly. 'You'd be surprised, little fellow. There's not much I cannot do.'

'Would you really do what I ask?' said Holger, really curious now.

'On my word of honour!' the devil swore, and took his left hoof in his hand, which meant the same to him as crossing our hearts does to us.

'Well, then,' said Holger, 'I wish that the devil who has been tormenting the village would fall head over heels down the mountain and never show his face here again.'

The devil had not expected this! But an oath is an oath and, cursing horribly, he fell head over heels down the mountain. He reached the bottom, bruised black and blue, and took himself off for good and all.

'I knew it was him all the time!' said little Holger.

He jumped down from the gate, picked up a feather that had dropped from the devil's cap when he fell, and planted it in his own torn hat.

From *The Devil in the Tower: Seven Diabolical Tales* by Johan Fabricius (Longman Young Books)
(See Note, page 167)

hist whist

hist   whist
little ghostthings
tip-toe
twinkle-toe

little twitchy
witches and tingling
goblins
hob-a-nob   hob-a-nob

little hoppy happy
toad in tweeds
tweeds
little itchy mousies

with scuttling
eyes   rustle and run   and
hidehidehide
whisk

whisk   look out for the old woman
with the wart on her nose
what she'll do to yer
nobody knows

for she knows the devil   ooch
the devil   ooch
the devil
ach   the great

green
dancing
devil
devil

devil
devil

wheeE E E

From *The Complete Poems of e. e. cummings* by
e. e. cummings
(MacGibbon & Kee Ltd)

The Duchess of Houndsditch

Once upon a time, in the days before there were such things as diesel engines and every train went by steam, there was an engine called the Duchess of Houndsditch, and she was as dear to her engine driver, William Bloggs, as a bicycle is to you. Every day he rubbed her brass trimmings till they shone like fairy lights, and he polished her plum-coloured sides till they glowed like red cough mixture. But his real pride was her whistle. As clear as a bell it was, and so moving that not a signal on the line could resist her.

It happened one day that the station master sent for William Bloggs, and said that in a few days' time a Very Important Person would be travelling on his line, and that the Duchess had been chosen to carry him, because of her musical toot.

William was delighted. Here at last was fame!

Now the Duchess had one failing. She was rather flighty, and she chose this of all times to start a grievance.

'Why,' she said to herself, 'must I, every day of my life, be fed on nothing but lumps of hard, knobbly coal, and green, greasy train-oil?'

As they bowled along through the outskirts of the town towards the open country, she got quite worked up about it.

'It's a shame, that's what it is,' she said to herself. 'Here I am bursting my boilers to give satisfaction, and for what? Coal and train-oil, day after day. If only I could have some . . .' and here she looked round rather vaguely, for she didn't really know what she wanted. By this time they were well out into the country. On either side of the track were wide pastures, lush with grass and yellow buttercups, on which cows were peacefully grazing.

'If only,' said the Duchess, 'if only I could browse on lush green grass and yellow buttercups.'

In a short time they stopped at their first station. It was a neat, well-kept station with the name marked in Virginia Stock in the flower-bed as well as written on the seats and placards.

William, like the porter of the station, was a keen gardener, and today, as on many days, he left the train for a few minutes' chat about his vegetable marrows. This gave the Duchess her chance; she had noticed beyond the signal-box a meadow, full of brown, contented cows, browsing peacefully on lush green grass and yellow buttercups. The station was empty except for the station cat stalking flies, and without thinking twice she undid her couplings, picked up her pistons, and crept quietly away. A few cows looked up in mild surprise when she lumbered rather heavily into the field. They had no objection, it seemed, to her joining them in a little lush grass and yellow buttercups.

'But chew your cud well, dear,' volunteered the nearest cow. 'Buttercups is bilious if you aren't used to them.'

The Duchess thanked the cow for her politeness, and did her best to appear as though she were enjoying her meal. She put away enough to make a small haystack, and then she decided that perhaps the kindly cow was right about buttercups. She was feeling rather queer. Back on her line, securely coupled once more, she felt better. As luck would have it, she got back just as

William Bloggs reappeared with a parcel of seedlings done up in damp newspaper.

Off they went once more, the Duchess a bit slow on her regulator, but all went well till they came to the next signal. William was anxious to make up for lost time, and this particular signal was the oldest and most obstinate on the line. It would hold up an express as soon as look at her. But William only smiled as he pulled the whistle cord. 'Now ask him nicely, old lady,' he said confidently.

There was a pause, but no whistle; only, from somewhere, so close that it might have come from the cab itself, came an unmistakable 'Moo!'

William Bloggs started. There was not a cow in sight. But why was it that the Duchess had not tooted? He pulled the cord again, harder this time, and again there came a prolonged and dismal 'Moo-o-o!'

The signal stood bolt upright in shocked amazement. Could it be that the rich colour of the Duchess's rounded sides flushed to a deeper crimson? With an anxious heart, William Bloggs waited till in its own time the signal at last deigned to go down and let them through.

That night, for the very first time, they were late. William drove the Duchess straight into her shed. Perhaps a night's rest would put her right.

Next morning she refused to touch either coal or train-oil. William clicked his tongue unhappily. The Duchess off her feed! Such a thing had never happened before. But at the usual time they set off again, and William hoped for the best.

The truth of the matter was that the Duchess was sulking. Not that she had enjoyed the buttercups, but there were other things in the world to eat, she said to herself, and there was William Bloggs giving her the same old coal and train-oil again. As the train climbed to higher ground, the buttercup fields became fewer, and their place was taken by meadows full of sorrel and round white daisies. There were no cows here, only soft sheep with frisking lambs in black woolly gaiters.

'That's what I want!' said the Duchess defiantly. 'Sorrel and round white daisies!'

She watched her chance. When the train stopped at the next station, William Bloggs went to pass the time of day with the signalman, whose wife brewed such excellent herb beer. The Duchess slipped away quietly and unobtrusively to the nearest field. The sheep were not as polite as the cows had been, and some of the lambs were downright cheeky. Defiantly the Duchess put away even more daisies than she had buttercups the day before, and so quickly that she was hiccuping slightly when she got back to the line. William Bloggs, wiping his mouth with the back of his hand, hoisted himself up into the cab a few minutes later.

Presently they came to the same obstinate signal. William put a nervous hand on the whistle cord, and pulled. There was a pause. Then, horror piled on horror, she did not whistle like an engine, or even moo like a cow. The only sound which met his ear was a long-drawn 'Ba-a-a!'

Again William Bloggs was late. This time he was seriously worried. What was he to do? In two days' time they were to carry the Very Important Person.

Next day William got out at the third station on the line and went to see the station master. His name was Perkins, and he was an old friend. William Bloggs had stood godfather to all the little Perkinses. The kitchen was bright and cheerful, with geraniums in the window, and a canary singing its head off in a cage. William found its whistle strangely comforting, because it reminded him of the Duchess's own lost voice. Mr Perkins chatted of this and that, but William was too worried to keep his mind on the conversation.

Presently Mrs Perkins said: 'Whoever's gone and let the hens out? They're all over the platform. And, William, wherever is your engine?'

William Bloggs rushed out. There was no sign of his beloved engine, only half a dozen hens scratching hopefully on the dusty platform. He looked wildly round; there in the little hen-run behind the station master's house was the Duchess of Houndsditch. She was watching a young cockerel very closely, and apparently trying to scratch up the ground with her back driving-wheels. Every now and then she ducked clumsily as a hen might to peck at a grain of corn.

'Duchess!' roared William Bloggs in a voice of thunder. The Duchess started guiltily. 'Get back to your line, Miss!' Now it was the first time that he had ever spoken harshly to her, and she was so surprised that she obeyed at once. As the train went on again, William Bloggs thought hard. Without waiting to reach the obstinate signal, he pulled the whistle cord, and it was just as he feared, the Duchess gave neither hoot, moo nor baa, but a loud 'Cock-a-doodle-doo!' William did some more thinking. She had been eating corn with a cock and now she crowed. Yesterday he had found bits of daisies in the cab as though someone had been playing she-loves-me-she-loves-me-not with the petals, and she had baa-ed like a sheep, and the day before that there had been a couple of battered buttercups sticking out of her safety valve, and she had moo-ed like a cow. Clearly if she was to make a respectable engine noise again, she must be persuaded to take proper train food. But might not that merely restore her voice to an ordinary everyday engine level? What could he give her to restore her whistle to all its old wild beauty? Somewhere at the back of his mind he remembered hearing a sound in Mr Perkins' kitchen which had been familiar and reassuring. Then he remembered, and his worried face relapsed into a smile.

That night he gave the Duchess no coal or oil. Instead, he talked to her very sternly about turning up her blast-nozzle at the good coal provided when many an engine would be glad of it. At first she twirled her bogie-wheels defiantly, and pretended that she didn't care. But presently she began to be ashamed of herself, for she was a good-hearted creature really and what's more, she was feeling very, very empty. It was a meek Duchess of Houndsditch who finally went to her shed that night.

The following morning William polished her brass work till she twinkled like the Milky Way; then he rubbed her sides till they glowed like stained glass with a sunset behind it. Next he gave her the finest and richest train-oil available, and a great heap of shining coal, every lump of which he had hand-picked himself, and mixed with the coal was a hundredweight of canary seed. William watched anxiously. It all disappeared; every drop of oil, every fragment of coal and grain of canary seed. What would be the result? But there was no time to waste in worrying, for they were due even now to meet the Very Important Person. Off they started, amid the click and whirr of cameras, the cheering of the crowds and the playing of the town band, past meadows full of cows and yellow buttercups: past the station where all the little Perkinses were lined up cheering and waving flags: past the hen-run, on and on, until they came to the difficult signal. Would it dare to hold up a train with a Very Important Person on board? But it did. With his heart in his mouth, William Bloggs put up a trembling hand, then: 'Let him have it, old lady!' he said, as he pulled the whistle cord, and the Duchess whistled. The sound rose true and steady in the morning air, neither moo, baa, nor crow, but an exquisite whistle which both compelled and enchanted at the same time.

The signal quivered and fell without protest. The Very Important Person so far forgot himself as to pop his head out of the window. William Bloggs sighed with relief. 'Good old Duchess!' he said, as she sped happily on to the terminus. There would be more crowds at the end of the journey: more speeches and more cameras, and who knows, even a microphone into which his darling Duchess might whistle to the listening millions!

From *West of Widdershins* by Barbara Sleigh
(Collins)
(See Note, page 167)

A Box on the Ear

On a cold winter's day a lad went tramping to look for work. He was hungry, he was ragged, he hadn't a penny, and he tramped on till evening. It was no night to sleep under a hedge, so he went to an inn and begged for shelter. But the landlord said they were expecting a great company that night, so ragged folk were not welcome. And he turned the lad away.

Well, the lad walked on for a bit, and then he saw a big house standing back from the road.

'Maybe I'll get a night's lodging in the kitchen here for a job of work in the morning,' thought he. So he opened the gate and walked up the drive.

But when he drew near the house, what was his surprise to see the front door flung violently open and a crowd of people rushing out: first the mistress of the house, then the master, and then all the servants, fairly tumbling over each other in their hurry to get away.

The lad stepped in front of the mistress, but she dodged round him, picked up her skirts and ran off down the drive. So then the

103

lad gave a skip and got in front of the master.

'Sir,' said he, 'I have a favour to ask.'

'Favour!' cried the master. 'This is not the time to ask for favours! Can't you see we're in a hurry to leave before the ghost comes?'

'Ah, but I've come to lay the ghost for you,' said the lad, bold as brass.

'If you can do that,' said the master, 'you shall have a bag full of gold!'

'I'd rather have a sausage to fry,' said the lad, 'for my stomach is empty and crying out.'

'Well, well, you'll find a sausage in the kitchen,' shouted the master. And he ran off down the drive, and out through the gate, and away along the road to the inn, followed by all the servants.

The lad went into the house and found his way to the kitchen. There were a few embers still smouldering on the hearth; and, yes, sure enough, there was a big sausage in a dish on a shelf.

The lad was so hungry that he ate a bit of the sausage raw. Then he threw wood on the hearth until the fire roared up, for he was very cold. And after that he cut the rest of the sausage into slices, and waited for the flames on the hearth to die down. When there were no more flames, but only glowing embers, he laid some slices of sausage on the embers to toast them, turning them carefully from time to time with the fire tongs.

Ah good, good! Soon he was munching a slice of hot sausage; and with a jug of beer that he found to wash down the meat— what could a lad ask more?

So, as he was munching away at that first slice, he heard a deep voice calling from out of the chimney, 'I fall! I fall!'

'Fall then!' said the lad with his mouth full. 'And if you fall in pieces, what do I care?'

And hardly had he said this when, *trip, trap,* down from the chimney fell the leg of a man. The leg hopped over the hot embers, and stood itself upright on the kitchen floor. But the lad took no notice. He went on munching his toasted sausage.

And very soon the voice from the chimney spoke again: 'I fall! I

'Fall then!' said the lad with his mouth full.

Trip, trap! Down from the chimney fell another leg, hopped over the hot embers, and stood itself upright on the floor beside its fellow.

The lad didn't so much as turn round. He picked another slice of sausage out of the embers, and went on eating.

'I fall, *I fall*, I FALL!' came the voice from the chimney, louder and louder.

'Fall then,' said the lad, biting off a huge piece of sausage. 'But why make such a fuss about it?'

Trip, trap! Down from the chimney fell the body of a man, bounced over the hot embers, and set itself up on top of the two legs.

The lad didn't look round. He went on eating.

'*I fall*, I FALL!' wailed the voice in the chimney.

'Fall then, and look sharp about it!' said the lad with his mouth full.

Trip, trap! Down from the chimney fell two arms, hopped over the hot embers and joined themselves to the ghost's body.

'It only wants its head now,' said the lad. He lifted another slice of sausage from the embers, and crammed it into his mouth; but he didn't look round at what stood behind him.

Then a voice came out of the chimney fairly roaring: 'I FALL! I FALL! I FALL!'

'Fall then and be done!' said the lad, with his mouth full of sausage.

And no sooner had he said that, when *trip, trap,* down from the chimney bounced a man's head, hopped over the hot embers, and set itself up on the body of the ghost.

The lad turned round then, looked the ghost full in its glaring eyes, and said, 'What do you want?'

The ghost didn't answer. It came and sat itself down by the fire close to the lad.

The lad took the tongs and lifted a slice of sausage off the embers. He was just about to eat that slice, when the ghost licked its fingers, covered its wet finger with ashes, and smeared the ashes all over the nicely toasted piece of sausage.

'If you do that again,' said the lad, 'I shall box your ears.'

And he laid another slice of sausage on the embers.

But when that slice was toasted and the lad lifted it off the embers, the ghost licked its fingers again, rubbed them in the ashes, and dirtied the slice of sausage all over.

So then the lad turned and gave the ghost such a box on the ear that it tumbled over on its back.

'And that will teach you to mind your manners,' said the lad.

The ghost got to its feet. It was laughing. 'Little brother, thank you! I have been seven years without rest because in life I felled my father with a box on the ear. No, I could not rest until someone did the like to me. Now I have taken the payment. And so good-bye! Goodbye!'

And when it had said that, the ghost laughed again, and vanished.

The lad went on with his cooking until he had toasted and eaten the last slice of sausage. Then he yawned, stretched himself out before the warm hearth, and slept.

In the morning the master and mistress and the servants came back to the house.

'The ghost has gone,' said the lad. 'He is on his way to heaven. He won't come here again.'

Then the master rejoiced and gave the lad a bag of gold. And the lad went merrily on his way.

From *A Book of Ghosts and Goblins*
by Ruth Manning-Sanders (Methuen Children's Books)
(See Note, page 168)

The Princess and the Pea

Once upon a time there was a prince who wanted to marry a princess, but she would have to be a real one. He travelled around the whole world looking for her; but every time he met a princess there was always something amiss. There were plenty of princesses but not one of them was quite to his taste. Something was always the matter: they just weren't real princesses. So he returned home very sad and sorry, for he had set his heart on marrying a real princess.

One evening a storm broke over the kingdom. The lightning flashed, the thunder roared, and the rain came down in bucketfuls. In the midst of this horrible storm, someone knocked on the city gate; and the king himself went down to open it.

On the other side of the gate stood a princess. But goodness, how wet she was! Water ran down her hair and clothes in streams. It flowed in through the heels of her shoes and out through the toes. But she said she was a real princess.

'We'll find that out quickly enough,' thought the old queen, but she didn't say a word out loud. She hurried to the guest room and took all the bedclothes off the bed; then on the bare bedstead she put a pea. On top of the pea she put twenty mattresses; and on top of the mattresses, twenty eiderdown quilts. That was the bed on which the princess had to sleep.

In the morning, when someone asked her how she had slept, she replied, 'Oh, just wretchedly! I didn't close my eyes once, the whole night through. God knows what was in that bed; but it was something hard, and I am black and blue all over.'

Now they knew that she was a real princess, since she had felt the pea that was lying on the bedstead through twenty mattresses and twenty eiderdown quilts. Only a real princess could be so sensitive!

The prince married her. The pea was exhibited in the royal museum; and you can go there and see it, if it hasn't been stolen.

Now that was a real story!

From *Hans Andersen: His Classic Fairytales*
Translated by Erik Haugaard (Gollancz)
(See Note, page 169)

The Simpleton

There was once a silly man, a simpleton, who set out to visit a friend in a distant village. He soon lost his way however, and asked a passer-by for the path to the village.

'The path goes up by that tree on the river bank,' answered the man.

The simpleton went on his way, but when he came to the tree, he *climbed up it*, for he thought the path must be up there. Hadn't the man said 'Up by that tree'? He climbed up and up until he was almost at the top, but still no path! Now he had reached the highest and thinnest branch. Crack! It broke under his weight and he fell through the branches, scattering twigs and leaves as he fell.

The gods be praised! Just as he thought he must fall into the river below, he managed to catch hold of a branch, first by one hand, then by both. He was safe—for the moment anyway.

'How pleasant it is up here!' he thought, as he swung gently to and fro. 'And how wet the river looks . . .'

But soon his arms began to tire and he grew afraid he would fall. 'Help! Help!' he cried. 'Help! Help!'

Now it happened that a man, a mahout, came by, riding on his elephant. He looked up in astonishment when he heard the cry for help. There he saw the simpleton in the tree, hanging from a branch by his hands.

'Hold on!' he shouted. 'I'll try to help you. Hold on a little longer!'

He guided his elephant so that it would pass right under the simpleton, stood on the elephant's back and caught hold of the simpleton's legs so as to lower him on to the animal's back.

But the elephant, confused and frightened by all this shouting, lumbered straight on so that its master's legs were dragged from under him and he was left hanging in space by the simpleton's legs, while the simpleton hung to the branch by his hands.

'Now we're in a fix!' said the mahout.

'How glad I am to have company!' said the simpleton happily. 'Can you sing? A song would pass the time.'

'Someone may hear if I sing loudly, and come to our help,' thought the mahout.

He began to sing with all his might while the simpleton listened admiringly.

'That's fine singing!' he exclaimed. 'You deserve a clap for that!'

And he let go of the branch to clap his hands!

What happened next? Why, they both fell into the river, of course. They haven't got out yet so I can't finish my story, can I?

Adapted by Eileen Colwell from an Indian folktale.
(See Note, page 170)

The Adventures of Isabel

Isabel met an enormous bear.
Isabel, Isabel didn't care;
The bear was hungry, the bear was ravenous,
The bear's mouth was cruel and cavernous.
The bear said, Isabel, glad to meet you,
How do, Isabel, now I'll eat you!
Isabel, Isabel, didn't worry,
Isabel didn't scream or scurry.
She washed her hands and she straightened her hair up,
Then Isabel quietly ate the bear up.

Once in a night as black as pitch
Isabel met a wicked witch.
The witch's face was cross and wrinkled,
The witch's gums with teeth were sprinkled.
Ho ho, Isabel! the old witch crowed,
I'll turn you into an ugly toad!
Isabel, Isabel, didn't worry,
Isabel didn't scream or scurry,
She showed no rage and she showed no rancour,
But she turned the witch into milk and drank her.

From *Many Long Years Ago*
by Ogden Nash (Dent)

The Fog Horn

Out there, in the cold water, far from land, we waited every night for the coming of the fog, and it came, and we oiled the brass machinery and lit the fog light up in the stone tower. Feeling like two birds in the grey sky, McDunn and I sent the light touching out, red, then white, then red again, to eye the lonely ships. And if they did not see our light, then there was always our voice, the great deep cry of our Fog Horn shuddering through the rags of mist to startle the gulls away like packs of scattered cards, and make the waves turn high and foam.

'It's a lonely life, but you're used to it now, aren't you?' asked McDunn.

'Yes,' I said. 'You're a good talker, thank the Lord.'

'Well, it's your turn on land tomorrow,' he said, smiling, 'to dance the ladies and drink gin.'

'What do you think, McDunn, when I leave you out here alone?'

'On the mysteries of the sea,' McDunn lit his pipe. It was a quarter past seven of a cold November evening, the heat on, the light switching its tail in two hundred directions, the Fog Horn

112

bumbling in the high throat of the tower. There wasn't a town for a hundred miles down the coast, just a road which came lonely through dead country to the sea, with few cars on it, a stretch of two miles of cold water out to our rock, and rare few ships.

'The mysteries of the sea,' said McDunn thoughtfully. 'You know, the ocean's the biggest damned snowflake ever? It rolls and swells a thousand shapes and colours, no two alike. Strange. One night, years ago, I was here all alone, when all the fish of the sea surfaced out there. Something made them swim in and lie in the bay, sort of trembling and staring up at the tower light going red, white, red, white across them so I could see their funny eyes. I turned cold. They were like a big peacock's tail, moving out there until midnight. Then, without so much as a sound, they slipped away, the million of them was gone. I kind of think maybe, in some sort of way, they came all those miles to worship. Strange. But think how the tower must look to them, standing seventy feet above the water, the God-light flashing out from it, and the tower declaring itself with a monster voice. They never came back, those fish, but don't you think for a while they thought they were in the Presence?'

I shivered. I looked out at the long grey lawn of the sea stretching away into nothing and nowhere.

'Oh, the sea's full.' McDunn puffed his pipe nervously blinking. He had been nervous all day and hadn't said why. 'For all our engines and so-called submarines, it'll be ten thousand centuries before we set foot on the real bottom of the sunken lands, in the fairy kingdoms there, and know real terror. Think of it, it's still the year 300,000 Before Christ down under there. While we've paraded around with trumpets, lopping off each other's countries and heads, they have been living beneath the sea twelve miles deep and cold in a time as old as the beard of a comet.'

'Yes, it's an old world.'

'Come on, I got something special I been saving up to tell you.'

We ascended the eighty steps, talking and taking our time. At the top McDunn switched off the room lights so there'd be no reflection in the plate glass. The great eye of the light was humming, turning easily in its oiled socket. The Fog Horn was blowing steadily, once every fifteen seconds.

'Sounds like an animal, don't it?' McDunn nodded to himself. 'A big lonely animal crying in the night. Sitting here on the edge of ten billion years calling out to the Deeps, I'm here, I'm here. And the Deeps *do* answer, yes, they do. You been here now for three months, Johnny, so I better prepare you. About this time of year,' he said, studying the murk and fog, 'something comes to visit the lighthouse.'

'The swarms of fish like you said?'

'No, this is something else. I've put off telling you because you might think I'm daft. But tonight's the latest I can put it off, for if my calendar's marked right from last year, tonight's the night it comes. I won't go into detail, you'll have to see it for yourself. Just sit down there. If you want, tomorrow you can pack your duffel and take the motorboat in to land and get your car parked there at the dinghy pier on the cape and drive on back to some little inland town and keep your lights burning nights, I won't question or blame you. It's happened three years now, and this is the only time anyone's been here with me to verify it. You wait and watch.'

Half an hour passed with only a few whispers between us. When we grew tired of waiting, McDunn began describing some of his ideas to me. He had some theories about the Fog Horn itself.

'One day many years ago a man walked along and stood in the sound of the ocean on a cold sunless shore and said, ''We need a voice to call across the water, to warn ships; I'll make one. I'll make a voice like all of time and all of the fog that ever was; I'll make a voice that is like an empty bed beside you all night long, and like an empty house when you open the door, and like trees in autumn with no leaves. A sound like the birds flying south, crying, and a sound like November wind and the sea on the hard, cold shore. I'll make a sound that's so alone that no one can miss it, that whoever hears it will weep in their souls, and hearths will seem warmer, and being inside will seem better to all who hear it in distant towns. I'll make me a sound and an apparatus and they'll call it a Fog Horn and whoever hears it will know the sadness of eternity and the briefness of life." '

The Fog Horn blew.

'I made up that story,' said McDunn quietly, 'to try to explain why this thing keeps coming back to the lighthouse every year. The Fog Horn calls it, I think, and it comes . . .'

'But—' I said.

'Ssst!' said McDunn. 'There!' He nodded out to the Deeps.

Something was swimming towards the lighthouse tower.

It was a cold night, as I have said; the high tower was cold, the light coming and going, and the Fog Horn calling and calling through the ravelling mist. You couldn't see far and you couldn't see plain, but there was the deep sea moving on its way about the night earth, flat and quiet, the colour of grey mud, and here were the two of us alone in the high tower, and there, far out at first, was a ripple, followed by a wave, a rising, a bubble, a bit of froth. And then, from the surface of the cold sea came a head, a large head, dark-coloured, with immense eyes, and then a neck. And then—not a body—but more neck and more! The head rose a full forty feet above the water on a slender and beautiful dark neck. Only then did the body, like a little island of black coral and shells and cray-fish, drip up from the subterranean. There was a flicker of tail. In all, from head to tip of tail, I estimated the monster at ninety or a hundred feet.

I don't know what I said. I said something.

'Steady, boy, steady,' whispered McDunn.

'It's impossible!' I said.

'No, Johnny, *we're* impossible. *It's* like it always was ten million years ago. *It* hasn't changed. It's *us* and the land what've changed, become impossible. *Us!*'

It swam slowly and with a great dark majesty out in the icy waters far away. The fog came and went about it, momentarily erasing its shape. One of the monster eyes caught and held and flashed back our immense light, red, white, red, white, like a disc held high and sending out a message in primeval code. It was as silent as the fog through which it swam.

'It's a dinosaur of some sort!' I crouched down, holding on to the stair rail.

'Yes, one of the tribe.'

'But they died out!'

'No, only hid away in the Deeps. Deep, deep down in the deepest Deeps. Isn't *that* a word now, Johnny, a real word, it says so much: the Deeps. There's all the coldness and darkness and deepness in the world in a word like that.'

'What'll we do?'

'Do? We got our job and we can't leave. Besides, we're safer here than in any boat trying to get to land. That thing's as big as a destroyer and almost as swift.'

'But here, why does it come *here*?'

The next moment I had my answer.

The Fog Horn blew.

And the monster answered.

A cry came across a million years of water and mist. A cry so anguished and alone that it shuddered in my head and my body. The monster cried out at the tower. The Fog Horn blew. The monster roared again. The Fog Horn blew. The monster opened its great toothed mouth and the sound that came from it was the sound of the Fog Horn itself. Lonely and vast and far away. The sound of isolation, a viewless sea, a cold night, apartness. That was the sound.

'Now!' whispered McDunn, 'do you know why it comes here?'

I nodded.

'All year long, Johnny, that poor monster there lying far out, a thousand miles at sea, and twenty miles deep maybe, biding in time, perhaps it's a million years old, this one creature. Think of it, waiting a million years; could *you* wait that long? Maybe it's the last of its kind. I sort of think that's true. Anyway, here come men on land and build this lighthouse, five years ago. And set up their Fog Horn and sound it and sound it out towards the place where you bury yourself in sleep, and sea memories of a world where there were thousands like yourself but now you're alone, all alone in a world where you have to hide.

'But the sound of the Fog Horn comes and goes, comes and goes, and you stir from the muddy bottom of the Deeps, and your eyes open like the lenses of two-foot cameras and you move, slow, slow, for you have the ocean sea on your shoulders, heavy. But that Fog Horn comes through a thousand miles of water, faint and familiar, and the furnace in your belly stokes up, and you begin to rise, slow, slow. You feed yourself on great slakes of cod and minnow, on rivers of jellyfish, and you rise slow, through the autumn months, through September when the fogs started, through October with more fog and the horn still calling you on, and then, late in November, after pressurising yourself day by day, a few feet higher every hour, you are near the surface and still alive. You've got to go slow; if you surfaced all at once you'd explode. So it takes you all of three months to surface, and then a number of days to swim through the cold waters to the light-house. And there you are, out there, in the night, Johnny, the biggest damn monster in creation, and here's the lighthouse calling to you, with a long neck sticking way up out of the water, and a body like your body and most important of all, a voice like your voice. Do you understand now, Johnny, do you under-stand?'

The Fog Horn blew.

The monster answered.

I saw it all, I knew it all—the million years of waiting alone, for someone to come back who never came back. The million years of isolation at the bottom of the sea, the insanity of time there, while the skies cleared of reptile birds, the swamps dried on the continental lands, the sloths and sabre-tooths had their day and sank in the tar pits, and men ran like white ants upon the hills.

The Fog Horn blew.

'Last year,' said McDunn, 'that creature swam round and round, round and round, all night. Not coming too near, puzzled, I'd say. Afraid, maybe. And a bit angry after coming all this way. But the next day, unexpectedly, the fog lifted, the sun came out fresh, the sky was blue as a painting. And the monster swam off

117

away from the heat and the silence and didn't come back. I suppose it's been brooding on it for a year now, thinking it over from every which way.'

The monster was only a hundred yards off now, it and the Fog Horn crying at each other. As the lights hit them, the monster's eyes were fire and ice, fire and ice.

'That's life for you,' said McDunn. 'Someone always waiting for someone who never comes home. Always someone loving something more than that thing loves them. And after a while you want to destroy whatever that thing is, so it can't hurt you no more.'

The monster was rushing at the lighthouse.

The Fog Horn blew.

'Let's see what happens,' said McDunn.

He switched the Fog Horn off.

The ensuing moment of silence was so intense that we could hear our hearts pounding in the glassed area of the tower, could hear the slow greased turn of the light.

The monster stopped and froze. Its great lantern eyes blinked. Its mouth gaped. It gave a sort of rumble, like a volcano. It twitched its head this way and that, as if to seek the sounds now dwindled off into the fog. It peered at the lighthouse. It rumbled again. Then its eyes caught fire. It reared up, threshed the water, and rushed at the tower, its eyes filled with angry torment.

'McDunn!' I cried. 'Switch on the horn!'

McDunn fumbled with the switch. But even as he flicked it on the monster was rearing up. I had a glimpse of its gigantic paws, fishskin glittering in webs beneath the fingerlike projections, clawing at the tower. The huge eye on the right side of its anguished head glittered before me like a cauldron into which I might drop, screaming. The tower shook. The Fog Horn cried; the monster cried. It seized the tower and gnashed at the glass, which shattered in upon us.

McDunn seized my arm. 'Downstairs!'

The tower rocked, trembled, and started to give. The Fog Horn and the monster roared. We stumbled and half fell down the stairs. 'Quick!'

118

We reached the bottom as the tower buckled down towards us. We ducked under the stairs into the small stone cellar. There were a thousand concussions as the rocks rained down; the Fog Horn stopped abruptly. The monster crashed upon the tower. The tower fell. We knelt together, McDunn and I, holding tight, while our world exploded.

Then it was over, and there was nothing but darkness and the wash of the sea on the raw stones.

That and the other sound.

'Listen,' said McDunn quietly. 'Listen.'

We waited a moment. And then I began to hear it. First a great vacuumed sucking of air, and then the lament, the bewilderment, the loneliness of the great monster, folded over and upon us, above us, so that the sickening reek of its body filled the air a stone's thickness away from our cellar. The monster gaped and cried. The tower was gone. The light was gone. The thing that had called to it across a million years was gone. And the monster was opening its mouth and sending out great sounds. The sounds of a Fog Horn, again and again. And ships far at sea, not finding the light, not seeing anything, but passing and hearing late that night, must've thought: There it is, the lonely sound, the Lonesome Bay horn. All's well. We've rounded the cape.

And so it went for the rest of that night.

The sun was hot and yellow the next afternoon when the rescuers came out to dig us from our stoned-under cellar.

'It fell apart, is all,' said McDunn gravely. 'We had a few bad knocks from the waves and it just crumbled.' He pinched my arm.

There was nothing to see. The ocean was calm, the sky blue. The only thing was a great algaic stink from the green matter that covered the fallen tower stones and the shore rocks. Flies buzzed about. The ocean washed empty on the shore.

The next year they built a new lighthouse, but by that time I had a job in the little town and a wife and a good small warm house that glowed yellow on autumn nights, the doors locked, the chimney puffing smoke. As for McDunn, he was master of the new lighthouse, built on his own specifications, out of steel-reinforced concrete. 'Just in case,' he said.

The new lighthouse was ready in November. I drove down alone one evening late and parked my car and looked across the grey waters and listened to the new horn sounding, once, twice, three, four times a minute far out there, by itself.

The monster?

It never came back.

'It's gone away,' said McDunn. 'It's gone back to the Deeps. It's learned you can't love anything too much in this world. It's gone into the deepest Deeps to wait another million years. Ah, the poor thing! Waiting out here, and waiting out there, while man comes and goes on this pitiful little planet. Waiting and waiting.'

I sat in my car, listening. I couldn't see the lighthouse or the light standing out in Lonesome Bay. I could only hear the Horn, the Horn, the Horn. It sounded like the monster calling.

I sat there wishing there was something I could say.

From *The Golden Apples of the Sun*
by Ray Bradbury. (Hart-Davis)
(See Note, page 171)

Schnitzle, Schnotzle and Schnootzle

The Tirol straddles the Alps and reaches one hand into Italy and another into Austria. There are more mountains in the Tirol than you can count and every Alp has its story.

Long ago, some say on the Brenner-Alp, some say on the Mitterwald-Alp, there lived the king of all the goblins of the Tirol, and his name was Laurin. King Laurin. His kingdom was under the earth, and all the gold and silver of the mountains he owned. He had a daughter, very young and very lovely, not at all like her father, who had a bulbous nose, big ears, and a squat figure and looked as old as the mountains. She loved flowers and was sad that none grew inside her father's kingdom.

'I want a garden of roses—red roses, pink roses, blush roses, flame roses, shell roses, roses like the sunrise and the sunset.' This she said one day to her father. And the king laughed and said she should have just such a garden. They would roof it with crystal, so that the sun would pour into the depths of the kingdom and make the roses grow lovely and fragrant. The garden was planted and every rare and exquisite rose bloomed in it. And so much colour they spread upwards on the mountains around that the snow caught it and the mortals living in the valley pointed at it with wonder. 'What is it that makes our Alps so rosy, so glowing?' they asked. And they spoke of it ever after as the alpenglow.

I have told you this that you might know what kind of goblin King Laurin was. He was merry, and he liked to play pranks and have fun. He liked to go abroad into the valleys where the mortals lived, or pop into a herdsman's hut halfway up the mountain. There were men who said they had seen him—that small squat figure with a bulbous nose and big ears, gambolling with the goats on a summer day. And now I begin my story. It is an old one that Tirolese mothers like to tell to their children.

Long ago there lived in one of the valleys a very poor cobbler indeed. His wife had died and left him with three children, little boys, all of them—Fritzl, Franzl, and Hansl. They lived in a hut so small there was only one room in it, and in that was the cobbler's bench, a hearth for cooking, a big bed full of straw, and on the wall racks for a few dishes, and, of course, there was a table with a settle and some stools. They needed few dishes or pans, for there was never much to cook or eat. Sometimes the cobbler would mend the Sunday shoes of a farmer, and then there was good goats' milk to drink. Sometimes he would mend the holiday shoes of the baker, and then there was the good long crusty loaf of bread to eat. And sometimes he mended the shoes of the butcher, and then there was the good stew, cooked with meat in the pot, and noodles, leeks and herbs. When the cobbler gathered the little boys around the table and they had said their grace, he would laugh and clap his hands and sometimes even dance. 'Ha-ha!' he would shout. 'Today we have the good . . . what? Ah-h . . . today we eat . . . Schnitzle, Schnotzle, and Schnootzle!'

With that he would swing the kettle off the hook and fill every bowl brimming full, and Fritzl, Franzl, and Hansl would eat until they had had enough. Ach, those were the good days—the days of having Schnitzle, Schnotzle, and Schnootzle. Of course, the cobbler was making up nonsense and nothing else, but the stew tasted so much better because of the nonsense.

Now a year came with every month following his brother on leaden feet. The little boys and the cobbler heard the month of March tramp out and April tramp in. They heard June tramp out and July tramp in. And every month marched heavier than his brother. And that was because war was amongst them again. War, with workers taking up their guns and leaving mothers and children to care for themselves as best they could; and there was scant to pay even a poor cobbler for mending shoes. The whole village shuffled to church with the soles flapping and the heels lopsided, and the eyelets and buttons and straps quite gone.

Summer—that was not so bad. But winter came and covered up the good earth, and gone were the roots, the berries, the sorrel, and the corn. The tramp of November going out and December coming in was very loud indeed. The little boys were quite sure that the two months shook the hut as they passed each other on the mountainside.

As Christmas grew near, the little boys began to wonder if there would be any feast for them, if there would be the good father dancing about the room and laughing 'Ha-ha!' and singing 'Ho-ho!' and saying: 'Now, this being Christmas Day we have the good . . . what?' And this time the little boys knew that they would never wait for their father to say it; they would shout themselves: 'We know—it is the good Schnitzle, Schnotzle, and Schnootzle!' Ach, how very long it was since their father had mended shoes for the butcher! Surely—surely—there would be need soon again, with Christmas so near.

At last came the Eve of Christmas. The little boys climbed along the beginnings of the Brenner-Alp, looking for faggots. The trees had shed so little that year, every branch was green and grew fast to its tree, so few twigs had snapped, so little was there of dead, dried brush to fill their arms.

Their father came in when they had a small fire started, blowing his whiskers free of icicles, slapping his arms about his

123

big body, trying to put warmth back into it. 'Na-na, nobody will have a shoe mended today. I have asked everyone. Still there is good news. The soldiers are marching into the village. The inn is full. They will have boots that need mending, those soldiers. You will see.' He pinched a cheek of each little boy; he winked at them and nodded his head. 'You shall see—tonight I will come home with . . . what?'

'Schnitzle, Schnotzle, and Schnootzle,' they shouted together, those three.

So happy were they they forgot there was nothing to eat for supper—not a crust, not a slice of cold porridge-pudding, not the smallest sup of goats' milk. 'Will the soldiers have money to pay you?' asked Fritzl the oldest.

'Not the soldiers perhaps, but the captains. There might even be a general. I will mend the boots of the soldiers for nothing, for after all what day is coming tomorrow! They fight for us, those soldiers; we mend for them, ja? But a general—he will have plenty of money.'

The boys stood about while their father put all his tools, all his pieces of leather into a rucksack; while he wound and wound and wound the woollen scarf about his neck, while he pulled the cap far down on his head. 'It will be a night to freeze the ears off you,' he said. 'Now bolt the door after me, keep the fire burning with a little at a time; and climb into the straw-bed and pull the quilt over you. And let no one in!'

He was gone. They bolted the door; they put a little on the fire; they climbed into the big bed, putting Hansl, the smallest, in the middle. They pulled up the quilt, such a thin quilt to keep out so much cold! Straight and still and close they lay, looking up at the little spot of light the fire made on the ceiling, watching their breath go upwards in icy spurts. With the going of the sun the wind rose. First it whispered: it whispered of good fires in big chimneys; it whispered of the pines on the mountainsides; it whispered of snow loosening and sliding over the glaciers. Then it began to blow: it blew hard, it blew quarrelsome, it blew cold and colder. And at last it roared. It roared its wintry breath through the cracks in the walls and under the door. And Fritzl, Franzl, and Hansl drew closer together and shivered.

'Whee . . . ooh . . . bang, bang! Whee . . . ooh . . . bang, bang!'

'Is it the wind or someone knocking?' asked Franzl.

'It is the wind,' said Fritz.

'Whee . . . ooh . . . knock, knock!'

'Is it the wind or someone knocking?' asked Hansl.

'It is the wind *and* someone knocking!' said Fritzl.

He rolled out of the bed and went to the window. It looked out directly on the path to the door. 'Remember what our father said: do not open it,' said Franzl.

But Fritzl looked and looked. Close to the hut, beaten against it by the wind, stood a little man no bigger than Hansl. He was pounding on the door. Now they could hear him calling: 'Let me in! I tell you, let me in!'

'Oh, don't, don't!' cried Hansl.

'I must,' said Fritzl. 'He looks very cold, the wind is tearing at him as a wolf tears at a young lamb.' And with that he drew the bolt and into the hut skipped the oddest little man they had ever seen. He had a great peaked cap tied onto his head with deer-thongs. He had a round red face out of which stuck a bulbous nose, like a fat plum on a pudding. He had big ears. And his teeth were chattering so hard they made the stools to dance. He shook his fist at the three little boys. 'Ach, kept me waiting. Wanted to keep all the good food, all the good fire to yourselves? Na-na, that is no kind of hospitality.'

He looked over at the little bit of a fire on the hearth, making hardly any heat in the hut. He looked at the empty table, not a bowl set or a spoon beside it. He took up the big pot, peered into it, turned it upside down to make sure nothing was clinging to the bottom, set it down with a bang. 'So—you have already eaten it all. Greedy boys. But if you have saved no feast for me, you can at least warm me.' With that he climbed into the big straw-bed with Franzl, and Hansl, with his cap still tied under his chin. Fritzl tried to explain that they had not been greedy, that there had never been any food, not for days, to speak of. But he was too frightened

125

of the little man, of his eyes as sharp and blue as ice, of his mouth so grumbling.

'Roll over, roll over,' the little man was shouting at the two in the bed. 'Can't you see I have no room? Roll over and give me my half of the quilt.'

Fritzl saw that he was pushing his brothers out of the bed. 'Na-na,' he said, trying to make peace with their guest. 'They are little, those two. There is room for all if we but lie quiet.' And he started to climb into the bed himself, pulling gently at the quilt that there might be a corner for him.

But the little man bounced and rolled about shouting: 'Give me room, give me more quilt. Can't you see I'm cold? I call this poor hospitality to bring a stranger inside your door, give him nothing to eat, and then grudge him bed and covering to keep him warm.' He dug his elbow into the side of skinny little Hansl.

'Ouch!' cried the boy.

Fritzl began to feel angry. 'Sir,' he said, 'sir, I pray you to be gentle with my little brother. And I am sorry there has been nothing to give you. But our father, the cobbler, has gone to mend shoes for the soldiers. When he returns we look for food. Truly, this is a night to feast and to share. So if you will but lie still until he comes I can promise you . . .'

The little man rolled over and stuck his elbow into Fritzl's ribs. 'Promise-promise. Na-na, what good is a promise? Come get out of bed and give me your place.' He drew up his knees, put his feet in the middle of Fritzl's back and pushed with great strength. The next moment the boy was spinning across the room. 'There you go,' roared the little man after him. 'If you must keep warm turn cartwheels, turn them fast.'

For a moment Fritzl stood sullenly by the small speck of fire. He felt bruised and very angry. He looked over at the bed. Sure enough, the greedy little man had rolled himself up in the quilt leaving only a short corner of it for the two younger boys. He had taken more than half of the straw for himself, and was even then pushing and digging at Hansl. He saw Franzl raise himself up and take the place of his littlest brother, that he should get the digs.

126

Brrr . . . it was cold! Before he knew it Fritzl was doing as he had been told, turning cartwheels round the room. He had rounded the table and was coming toward the bed when—plop! Plop-plop-plop! Things were falling out of his pockets every time his feet swung high over his head. Plop-plop-plop! The two younger boys were sitting up in bed. It was their cries of astonishment which brought Fritzl's feet back to the floor again, to stay. In a circle about the room, he had left behind him a golden trail of oranges. Such oranges—big as two fists! And sprinkled everywhere between were comfits wrapped in gold and silver paper. Fritzl stood and gaped at them.

'Here, you, get out and warm yourself!' shouted the little man as he dug Franzl in the ribs. 'Cartwheels for you, boy!' And the next moment Franzl was whirling in cartwheels about the room. Plop-plop-plop! Things were dropping out of his pockets. Christmas buns, Christmas cakes covered with icing, with plums, with anise and caraway seeds.

The little man was digging Hansl now in the ribs. 'Lazy boy, greedy boy. Think you can have the bed to yourself now? Na-na, I'll have it! Out you go!' And he put his feet against the littlest boy's back and pushed him out onto the floor. 'Cartwheels . . .' he began; but Fritzl, forgetting his amazement at what was happening, shouted: 'But, sir, he is too little. He cannot turn . . .'

'Hold him up in the corner, then. You keep warmer when your heels are higher than your head. Step lively there. Take a leg, each of you, and be quick about it.'

So angry did the little man seem, so fiery and determined, that Fritzl and Franzl hurried their little brother over to the chimney corner, stood him on his head and each held a leg. Donner and Blitzen! What happened then! Whack-whack-whickety-whack! whack-whack-whickety-whack! Pelting the floor like hail against the roof came silver and gold pieces, all pouring out of Hansl's pockets.

Fritzl began to shout, Franzl began to dance. Hansl began to shout: 'Let me down, let me down!' When they did the three little boys danced around the pile, taking hands, singing 'Tra-la-la,'

127

and 'Fiddle-de-dee,' and 'Ting-a-ling-a-ling,' until their breath was gone, and they could dance no longer. They looked over at the bed and Fritzl was opening his mouth to say: 'Now, if you please, sir, we can offer you some Christmas cheer . . .' But the bed was empty, the quilt lay in a heap on the floor. The little man had gone.

The three little boys were gathering up the things on the floor—putting oranges into the big wooden bowl, buns and cakes on to the two platters, silver and gold pieces into this dish and that. And right in the midst of it all in came their father, stamping and puffing in through the door. He had brought bread, he had brought milk, he had brought meat for the good stew—and noodles.

Such a wonder, such a clapping of hands, such a singing as they worked to get ready the Christmas feast! Fritzl began the story about their Christmas guest; Franzl told it mid-through; but little Hansl finished, making his brothers stand him in the corner again on his head to show just how it was that all the silver and gold had tumbled out of his pockets.

'Na-na,' said the cobbler, 'we are the lucky ones. I did not know it was true; always I thought it was a tale the grandfathers told their children. The saying goes that King Laurin comes every year at the Christmas to one hut—one family—to play his tricks and share his treasure hoard.'

'He was a very ugly little man,' said Hansl. 'He dug us in our ribs and took all the bed for himself.'

'That was the king—that is the way he plays at being fierce. Say: "*Komm, Herr Jesus, und sei unser Gast,*" then draw up the stools. Ah-h . . . what have we to eat?'

The little boys shouted the answer all together: 'Schnitzle—Schnotzle—and Schnootzle!'

From *The Long Christmas* by Ruth Sawyer
(Bodley Head)
(See Note, page 172)

Baba Yaga and the
Little Girl with the Kind Heart

Once upon a time there was a widowed old man who lived alone in a hut with his little daughter. Very merry they were together, and they used to smile at each other over a table just piled with bread and jam. Everything went well, until the old man took it into his head to marry again.

Yes, the old man became foolish in the years of his old age, and he took another wife. And so the poor little girl had a stepmother. And after that everything changed. There was no more bread and jam on the table, and no more playing bo-peep, first this side of the samovar and then that, as she sat with her father at tea. It was worse than that, for she never did sit at tea. The stepmother said that everything that went wrong was the little girl's fault. And the old man believed his new wife, and so there were no more kind words for his little daughter. Day after day the stepmother used to say that the little girl was too naughty to sit at table. And then she would throw her a crust and tell her to get out of the hut and go and eat it somewhere else.

And the poor little girl used to go away by herself into the shed in the yard, and wet the dry crust with her tears, and eat it all alone. Ah me! she often wept for the old days, and she often wept at the thought of the days that were to come.

Mostly she wept because she was all alone, until one day she found a little friend in the shed. She was hunched up in a corner of the shed, eating her crust and crying bitterly, when she heard a little noise. It was like this: scratch-scratch. It was just that, a little grey mouse who lived in a hole.

Out he came, his little pointed nose and his long whiskers, his little round ears and his bright eyes. Out came his little humpy body and his long tail. And then he sat up on his hind legs, and curled his tail twice round himself and looked at the little girl.

The little girl, who had a kind heart, forgot all her sorrows, and took a scrap of her crust and threw it to the little mouse. The mouseykin nibbled and nibbled, and then it was gone, and he was looking for another. She gave him another bit, and presently that was gone, and another and another, until there was no crust left for the little girl. Well, she didn't mind that. You see, she was so happy seeing the little mouse nibbling and nibbling.

When the crust was done, the mouseykin looks up at her with his little bright eyes, and 'Thank you,' he says, in a little squeaky voice. 'Thank you,' he says; 'you are a kind little girl, and I am only a mouse, and I've eaten all your crust. But there is one thing I can do for you, and that is to tell you to take care. The old woman in the hut (and that was the cruel stepmother) is own sister to Baba Yaga, the bony-legged, the witch. So if ever she sends you on a message to your aunt, you come and tell me. For Baba Yaga would eat you soon enough, with her iron teeth if you did not know what to do.'

'Oh, thank you,' said the little girl; and just then she heard her stepmother calling to her to come in and clean up the tea things, and tidy the house, and brush the floor, and clean everybody's boots.

So off she had to go.

When she went in she had a good look at her stepmother, and sure enough she had a long nose, and she was as bony as a fish with all the flesh picked off, and the little girl thought of Baba Yaga and shivered, though she did not feel so bad when she remembered the mouseykin out there in the shed in the yard.

The very next morning it happened. The old man went off to pay a visit to some friends of his in the next village, and as soon as the old man was out of sight the wicked stepmother called the little girl.

'You are to go today to your dear little aunt in the forest,' says she, 'and ask her for a needle and thread to mend a shirt.'

'But here is a needle and thread,' says the little girl.

'Hold your tongue,' says the stepmother, and she gnashes her teeth, and they make a noise like clattering tongs. 'Hold your tongue,' she says. 'Didn't I tell you you are to go today to your dear little aunt to ask for a needle and thread to mend a shirt?'

'How shall I find her?' says the little girl, nearly ready to cry, for she knew that her aunt was Baba Yaga, the bony-legged, the witch.

The stepmother took hold of the little girl's nose and pinched it. 'That is your nose,' she says. 'Can you feel it?'

'Yes,' says the poor little girl.

'You must go along the road into the forest till you come to a fallen tree; then you must turn to your left, and then follow your nose and you will find her,' says the stepmother. 'Now, be off with you, lazy one. Here is some food for you to eat on the way.' She gave the little girl a bundle wrapped up in a towel.

The little girl wanted to go into the shed to tell the mouseykin she was going to Baba Yaga, and to ask what she should do. But she looked back, and there was the stepmother at the door watching her. So she had to go straight on.

She walked along the road through the forest till she came to the fallen tree. Then she turned to the left. Her nose was still hurting where the stepmother had pinched it, so she knew she had to go straight ahead. She was just setting out when she heard a little noise under the fallen tree.

'Scratch-scratch.'

And out jumped the little mouse, and sat up in the road in front of her.

'O mouseykin, mouseykin,' says the little girl, 'my stepmother has sent me to her sister. And that is Baba Yaga, the bony-legged, the witch, and I do not know what to do.'

'It will not be difficult,' says the little mouse, 'because of your kind heart. Take all the things you find in the road, and do with them what you like. Then you will escape from Baba Yaga, and everything will be well.'

'Are you hungry, mouseykin?' said the little girl.

'I could nibble, I think,' says the little mouse.

The little girl unfastened the towel, and there was nothing in it but stones. That was what the stepmother had given the little girl to eat by the way.

'Oh, I'm so sorry,' says the little girl. 'There's nothing for you to eat.'

'Isn't there?' said mouseykin, and as she looked at them the little girl saw the stones turn to bread and jam. The little girl sat down on the fallen tree, and the little mouse sat beside her, and they ate bread and jam until they were not hungry any more.

'Keep the towel,' says the little mouse. 'I think it will be useful. And remember what I said about the things you find on the way. And now goodbye,' says he.

'Goodbye,' says the little girl and runs along.

As she was running along she found a nice new handkerchief lying in the road. She picked it up and took it with her. Then she found a little bottle of oil. She picked it up and took it with her. Then she found some scraps of meat.

'Perhaps I'd better take them too,' she said; and she took them.

Then she found a gay blue ribbon, and she took that. Then she found a little loaf of good bread, and she took that too.

'I daresay somebody will like it,' she said.

And then she came to the hut of Baba Yaga, the bony-legged, the witch. There was a high fence round it with big gates. When she pushed them open they squeaked miserably, as if it hurt them to move. The little girl was sorry for them.

'How lucky,' she says, 'that I picked up the bottle of oil!' and she poured the oil into the hinges of the gates.

Inside the railings was Baba Yaga's hut, and it stood on hen's legs and walked about the yard. And in the yard there was standing Baba Yaga's servant, and she was crying bitterly because of the tasks Baba Yaga set her to do. She was crying bitterly and wiping her eyes on her petticoat.

'How lucky,' says the little girl, 'that I picked up a handkerchief!' And she gave the handkerchief to Baba Yaga's servant, who wiped her eyes on it and smiled through her tears.

Close by the hut was a huge dog, very thin, gnawing a dry crust.

'How lucky,' says the little girl, 'that I picked up a loaf!' And she gave the loaf to the dog, and he gobbled it up and licked his lips.

The little girl went bravely up to the hut and knocked on the door.

'Come in,' says Baba Yaga.

The little girl went in and there was Baba Yaga, the bony-legged, the witch, sitting weaving at a loom. In a corner of the hut was a thin black cat watching a mouse-hole.

'Good-day to you, auntie,' says the little girl, trying not to tremble.

'Good-day to you, niece,' says Baba Yaga.

'My stepmother has sent me to you to ask for a needle and thread to mend a shirt.'

'Very well,' says Baba Yaga, smiling, and showing her iron teeth. 'You sit down here at the loom, and go on with my weaving, while I go and get you the needle and thread.'

The little girl sat down at the loom and began to weave.

Baba Yaga went out and called to her servant, 'Go, make the bath hot, and scrub my niece. Scrub her clean. I'll make a dainty meal of her.'

The servant came in for the jug. The little girl begged her, 'Be

not too quick in making the fire, and carry the water in a sieve.'
The servant smiled, but said nothing, because she was afraid of
Baba Yaga. But she took a very long time about getting the bath
ready.

Baba Yaga came to the window and asked: 'Are you weaving,
little niece? Are you weaving, my pretty?'

'I am weaving, auntie,' says the little girl.

When Baba Yaga went away from the window, the little girl
spoke to the thin black cat who was watching the mouse-hole.

'What are you doing, thin black cat?'

'Watching for a mouse,' says the thin black cat. 'I haven't had
any dinner for three days.'

'How lucky,' says the little girl, 'that I picked up the scraps of
meat!' and she gave them to the thin black cat. The thin black cat
gobbled them up, and said to the little girl,—

'Little girl, do you want to get out of this?'

'Catkin dear,' says the little girl, 'I do want to get out of this, for
Baba Yaga is going to eat me with her iron teeth.'

'Well,' says the cat, 'I will help you.'

Just then Baba Yaga came to the window.

'Are you weaving, little niece?' she asked. 'Are you weaving,
my pretty?'

'I am weaving, auntie,' says the little girl, working away, while
the loom went clickety clack, clickety clack.

Baba Yaga went away.

Says the thin black cat to the little girl: 'You have a comb in
your hair, and you have a towel. Take them and run for it while
Baba Yaga is in the bath-house. When Baba Yaga chases after you,
you must listen; and when she is close to you, throw away the
towel, and it will turn into a big, wide river. It will take her a little
time to get over that. But when she does, you must listen; and as
soon as she is close to you throw away the comb, and it will sprout
up into such a forest that she will never get through it at all.'

'But she'll hear the loom stop,' says the little girl.

'I'll see to that,' says the thin black cat.

The cat took the little girl's place at the loom. ·

Clickety clack, clickety clack; the loom never stopped for a moment.

The little girl looked to see that Baba Yaga was in the bath-house, and then she jumped down from the little hut on hen's legs, and ran to the gate as fast as her legs could flicker.

The big dog leapt up to tear her to pieces. Just as he was going to spring on her he saw who she was.

'Why, this is the little girl who gave me the loaf,' says he. 'A good journey to you, little girl;' and he lay down again with his head between his paws.

When she came to the gates they opened quietly, quietly, without making any noise at all, because of the oil she had poured into their hinges.

Outside the gates there was a little birch tree that beat her in the eyes so that she could not go by.

'How lucky,' says the little girl, 'that I picked up the ribbon!' And she tied up the birch tree with the pretty blue ribbon. And the birch tree was so pleased with the ribbon that it stood still, admiring itself, and let the little girl go by.

How she did run!

Meanwhile the thin black cat sat at the loom. Clickety clack, clickety clack, sang the loom; but you never saw such a tangle as the tangle made by the thin black cat.

And presently Baba Yaga came to the window.

'Are you weaving, little niece?' she asked. 'Are you weaving, my pretty?'

'I am weaving, auntie,' says the thin black cat, tangling and tangling, while the loom went clickety clack, clickety clack.

'That's not the voice of my little dinner,' says Baba Yaga, and she jumped into the hut, gnashing her iron teeth; and there was no little girl, but only the thin black cat sitting at the loom, tangling and tangling the threads.

'Grr,' says Baba Yaga, and jumps for the cat, and begins banging it about. 'Why didn't you tear the little girl's eyes out?'

'In all the years I have served you,' says the cat, 'you have only given me one little bone; but the kind little girl gave me scraps of meat.'

135

Baba Yaga threw the cat into a corner, and went out into the yard.

'Why didn't you squeak when she opened you?' she asked the gates.

'Why didn't you tear her to pieces?' she asked the dog.

'Why didn't you beat her in the face, and not let her go by?' she asked the birch tree.

'Why were you so long in getting the bath ready? If you had been quicker, she never would have got away,' said Baba Yaga to the servant.

And she rushed about the yard, beating them all, and scolding at the top of her voice.

'Ah!' said the gates, 'in all the years we have served you, you never even eased us with water; but the kind little girl poured good oil into our hinges.'

'Ah!' said the dog, 'in all the years I've served you, you never threw me anything but burnt crusts; but the kind little girl gave me a good loaf.'

'Ah!' said the little birch tree, 'in all the years I've served you, you never tied me up, even with thread; but the kind little girl tied me up with a gay blue ribbon.'

'Ah!' said the servant, 'in all the years I've served you, you have never given me even a rag; but the kind little girl gave me a pretty handkerchief.'

Baba Yaga gnashed at them with her iron teeth. Then she jumped into the mortar and sat down. She drove it along with the pestle, and swept up her tracks with a besom, and flew off in pursuit of the little girl.

The little girl ran and ran. She put her ear to the ground and listened. Bang, bang, bangety bang! she could hear Baba Yaga beating the mortar with the pestle. Baba Yaga was quite close. There she was, beating with the pestle and sweeping with the broom, coming along the road.

As quickly as she could, the little girl took out the towel and threw it on the ground. And the towel grew bigger and bigger, and wetter and wetter, and there was a deep, broad river between

Baba Yaga and the little girl.

The little girl turned and ran on. How she ran!

Baba Yaga came flying up in the mortar. But the mortar could not float in the river with Baba Yaga inside. She drove it in, but only got wet for her trouble. Tongs and pokers tumbling down a chimney are nothing to the noise she made as she gnashed her iron teeth. She turned home, and went flying back to the little hut on hen's legs. Then she got together all her cattle and drove them to the water.

'Drink, drink!' she screamed to them; and the cattle drank all the river to the last drop. And Baba Yaga, sitting in the mortar, drove it with the pestle, and swept up her tracks with the besom, and flew over the dry bed of the river and on in pursuit of the little girl.

The little girl put her ear to the ground and listened. Bang, bang, bangety bang! She could hear Baba Yaga beating the mortar with the pestle. Nearer and nearer came the noise, and there was Baba Yaga, beating with the pestle and sweeping with the broom, coming along the road close behind.

The little girl threw down the comb, and it grew bigger and bigger, and its teeth sprouted up into a thick forest, so thick that not even Baba Yaga could force her way through. And Baba Yaga, gnashing her teeth and screaming with rage and disappointment, turned round and drove away home to her little hut on hen's legs.

The little girl ran on home. She was afraid to go in and see her stepmother, so she ran into the shed. Scratch, scratch! Out came the little mouse.

'So you got away all right, my dear,' says the little mouse. 'Now run in. Don't be afraid. Your father is back, and you must tell him all about it.'

The little girl went into the house.

'Where have you been?' says her father; 'and why are you so out of breath?'

The stepmother turned yellow when she saw her, and her eyes glowed, and her teeth ground together until they broke.

But the little girl was not afraid, and she went to her father and

137

climbed on his knee, and told him everything that had happened. And when the old man knew that the stepmother had sent his little daughter to be eaten by Baba Yaga, he was so angry that he drove her out of the house, and ever afterwards lived alone with the little girl. Much better it was for both of them.

The little mouse came and lived in the hut, and every day it used to sit up on the table and eat crumbs, and warm its paws on the little girl's glass of tea.

From *Old Peter's Russian Tales*
by Arthur Ransome
(Hamish Hamilton Children's Books)
(See Note, page 172)

The Rainbow
An Aboriginal story

'*Arvalla, arvalla. Yirnan yarra tukurpa yirripura.*' (Listen, listen, I have a story to pass on to you.) In the beginning was Bunylda, the spirit of the desert. And Bunylda lived in the salt-pans with his six-year-old daughter, Lolari. The salt-pans were dull and dry, and Lolari soon grew tired of the spinifex and the withered grass which were all that she had to play with, and she begged her uncle, Tyeera (the spirit of the wind) to take her to a place where there were flowers. So Tyeera picked her up and carried her across mile after hundred mile of desert until they came to a rain forest. Here he left her, saying, 'Be good. And I will come back for you in the evening.'

Lolari walked through the forest admiring the flowers and was happy. She had never seen such wonderful colours: the gossamer cloud of orchids, the wax-white veils of clematis, the crimson of the fire-flame, the golden waterfalls of wattle and the vivid blue of the jacarandas. She was enthralled. And tempted: tempted to pick the blooms. They will be so pretty to play with, she told herself, back in the desert. So she picked and picked until she could carry no more; then, her flowers in her arms, she sat down by the side of a stream to wait for her uncle.

But Mungolo, the guardian of the rain forest, noticed that some of his flowers were missing. On hands and knees he followed the trail of broken twigs and bent grass, till he came to Lolari sitting, the flowers in her lap, at the side of the stream. 'Wicked girl,' Mungolo shouted, 'to steal the jewels from my forest. I shall lock you for ever in the hollow trunk of a kurrajung!'

Lolari was terrified. She screamed. And her uncle, hearing her, came swooping down and seized her just in time, and bore her away through the bloodwoods and the casuarinas. But Mungolo was not to be thwarted so easily. He plucked a trumpet of convolvulus flower and blew the alarm; and with angry roar the spirits of the rain forest sprang into the air in pursuit. In an instant the sky was filled with sound and fury: first the frightened rushing of the wind, then the great dark cloud of the rain people. All evening the chase went on; till in the end the wind outstripped the rain, and Lolari was returned to her home in the salt-pans.

But her flowers were gone. So fast had Tyeera been forced to travel that the fire-flame, wattle and jacarandas had been torn one by one from the little girl's grasp and strewn in a great multicoloured arch across the sky: the rainbow, which to this day springs to life whenever the flowers are watered by rain and warmed by sun.

From *A Walk to the Hills of the Dreamtime* by James Vance Marshall
(Hodder & Stoughton)
(See Note, page 174)

The Magic Drum

A story from Japan

Once upon a time there lived in a Japanese village a man named Gengoro. Gengoro had a magic drum. When he beat one side of the drum saying, 'Long be the nose, long be the nose!' the nose became long, whoever it belonged to. When he beat the other side of the drum saying, 'Short be the nose, short be the nose!' the nose became short. But the drum must never be used just for fun. Its magic was only for making people happy and contented.

Gengoro would beat the drum for those who wanted their noses a little longer, or for those who wanted their noses a little shorter, and thus he made many people happy, for the size of your nose makes a lot of difference to your looks.

Now Gengoro was very curious about all sorts of things. So, after a time, he began to wonder how far a human nose could be stretched, *his* for instance. So one fine day when he had nothing else to do, he went out into the fields with his drum and beat it *r-r-*

rumti-tum . . . r-r-r-rumti-tum . . . saying 'Long be *my* nose, long be *my* nose!'

Immediately Gengoro's nose began to stretch. Soon it was as long as his arm. Gengoro kept on drumming *r-r-r-rumti-tum . . . r-r-r-rumti-tum* . . . and saying 'Long be my nose, long be my nose!'

Soon his nose became as long as a pole to carry things with. But Gengoro did not stop for a moment. He beat the drum and said again and again, 'Long be my nose, long be my nose!'

Before long his nose was as long as a clothes-line. It grew so heavy also that Gengoro overbalanced. But he lay down on the ground with his nose towards the sky and went on beating the drum, *r-r-r-rumti-tum . . . r-r-r-rumti-tum* . . . and saying 'Long be my nose, long be my nose!'

His nose stretched and stretched and stretched. It went up higher than the trees, higher than the highest mountains, until its tip disappeared into a white cloud far up in the sky.

Just at that moment, the carpenters in the heavens were building a bridge between the stars called the Milky Way. Suddenly Gengoro's nose appeared, right on the spot where an old carpenter was fixing the railing of the bridge. The old man had no idea that this was a man's nose. He thought it was merely one of the pieces of wood he was using to make the bridge. So he tied it firmly to the railing with a piece of string.

Meanwhile, Gengoro on the earth felt something was wrong with his nose. Though he was still beating the drum, his nose wasn't stretching any longer. Besides the tip of his nose was tickling.

'I'd better shorten my nose again and see what's happened, 'he said to himself, and this time he beat the other side of the drum *r-r-r-rumti-tum . . . r-r-r-rumti-tum* . . . and said 'Short be my nose, short be my nose!'

But alas . . . Gengoro's nose was fastened to the railing of the bridge. So, when his nose began to shrink, instead of his nose coming down, his body went up!

'Good heavens!' he cried. 'Somebody is trying to steal my nose. I must hurry and get to the end of it to see what is happening!' *r-r-*

r-rumti-tum . . . r-r-r-rumti-tum . . . He beat the drum for dear life.

When he reached the sky at last, nobody was to be seen on the Milky Way, for it was noon and all the workmen had gone for lunch. When Gengoro found out what had happened to his nose, he was most annoyed.

'Well, really!' he exclaimed. 'Somebody has mistaken my nose for a piece of wood. How stupid some people are!' He untied his nose from the railing and tenderly pressed it into a good shape again.

Now he felt much better. But without that long, long nose, how could he get back to the earth? He looked down from the bridge but there was nothing to see but white clouds.

At that very moment the clouds beneath the bridge parted and through the gap he saw a blue lake far below. It was so far down that Gengoro felt terribly dizzy, so dizzy that—*oooops!* he fell from the bridge head over heels.

Splash! He found himself in a big lake called Lake Biwa in the country of Omi. He tried to swim but something was wrong with his body. He had lost his arms and legs. Instead he now had small fins and a tail. His mouth and nose had become pointed too—just like a fish! Yes, he had been turned into a fish as a punishment for using the magic drum just for fun.

If you go to Lake Biwa today, you will see many little fish like Gengoro. What are they called? Why, Gengoro-fish, of course!

By Momoko Ishii. Translated by Kyoko Matsuoka and adapted by Eileen Colwell (Iwanami Shoten, Tokyo)
(See Note, page 174)

What did you put in your Pocket?

What did you put in your pocket
What did you put in your pocket
   in your pockety pockety pocket
Early Monday morning?

I put in some chocolate pudding
I put in some chocolate pudding
   slushy glushy pudding
Early Monday morning.

Refrain: SLUSHY GLUSHY PUDDING!

What did you put in your pocket
What did you put in your pocket
   in your pockety pockety pocket
Early Tuesday morning?

I put in some ice-cold water
I put in some ice-cold water
   nicy icy water
Early Tuesday morning.

Refrain: SLUSHY GLUSHY PUDDING!
         NICY ICY WATER!

What did you put in your pocket
What did you put in your pocket
   in your pockety pockety pocket
Early Wednesday morning?

I put in a scoop of ice cream
I put in a scoop of ice cream
  slurpy glurpy ice cream
Early Wednesday morning.

Refrain: SLUSHY GLUSHY PUDDING!
           NICY ICY WATER!
           SLURPY GLURPY ICE CREAM!

What did you put in your pocket
What did you put in your pocket
  in your pockety pockety pocket
Early Thursday morning?

I put in some mashed potatoes
I put in some mashed potatoes
  fluppy gluppy potatoes
Early Thursday morning.

Refrain: SLUSHY GLUSHY PUDDING!
           NICY ICY WATER!
           SLURPY GLURPY ICE CREAM!
           FLUPPY GLUPPY POTATOES!

What did you put in your pocket
What did you put in your pocket
  in your pockety pockety pocket
Early Friday morning?

I put in some sticky treacle
I put in some sticky treacle
  sticky icky treacle
Early Friday morning.

Refrain: SLUSHY GLUSHY PUDDING!
      NICY ICY WATER!
      SLURPY GLURPY ICE CREAM!
      FLUPPY GLUPPY POTATOES!
      STICKY ICKY TREACLE!

What did you put in your pocket
What did you put in your pocket
  in your pockety pockety pocket
Early Saturday morning?

I put in my five fingers
I put in my five fingers
  funny finny fingers
Early Saturday morning.

Refrain: SLUSHY GLUSHY PUDDING!
      NICY ICY WATER!
      SLURPY GLURPY ICE CREAM!
      FLUPPY GLUPPY POTATOES!
      STICKY ICKY TREACLE!
      FUNNY FINNY FINGERS!

What did you put in your pocket
What did you put in your pocket
  in your pockety pockety pocket
Early Sunday morning?

I put in a clean white handkerchief
I put in a clean white handkerchief
  a spinky spanky handkerchief
Early Sunday morning.

146

WHAT DID YOU PUT IN YOUR POCKET

Refrain: SLUSHY GLUSHY PUDDING!

NICY ICY WATER!

SLURPY GLURPY ICE CREAM!

FLUPPY GLUPPY POTATOES!

STICKY ICKY TREACLE!

FUNNY FINNY FINGERS!

SPINKY SPANKY HANDKERCHIEF!

From *Something Special*
by Beatrice Schenk de Regniers (Collins)

A Christmas Story

This is the story the gipsy mothers tell their children on the night of Christmas, as they sit round the fire that is always burning in the heart of a Romany camp.

It was winter—and twelve months since the gipsies had driven their flocks of mountain-sheep over the dark, gloomy Balkans, and had settled in the southlands near to the Aegean. It was twelve months since they had seen a wonderful star appear in the sky and heard the singing of angelic voices afar off.

They had marvelled much concerning the star until a runner had passed them from the South bringing them news that the star had marked the birth of a Child whom the wise men had hailed as 'King of Israel' and 'Prince of Peace'. This had made Herod of Judea both afraid and angry and he had sent soldiers secretly to kill the Child; but in the night they had miraculously disappeared—the Child with Mary and Joseph—and no one knew whither they had gone. Therefore Herod had sent runners all over the lands that bordered the Mediterranean with a message forbidding everyone to give food or shelter or warmth to the Child, under penalty of death. For Herod's anger was far-reaching and where his anger fell there fell his sword likewise. Having given his warning, the runner passed on, leaving the gipsies to marvel much over the tale they had heard and the meaning of the star.

Now on that day that marked the end of the twelve months since the star had shone the gipsies said among themselves: 'Dost thou think that the star will shine again tonight? If it were true, what the runner said, that when it shone twelve months ago it marked the place where the Child lay, it might even mark his hiding-place this night. Then Herod would know where to find Him, and send his soldiers again to slay Him. That would be a cruel thing to happen!'

The air was chill with the winter frost, even there in the southland, close to the Aegean; and the gipsies built high their fire and hung their kettle full of millet, fish and bitter herbs for their supper. The king lay on his couch of tiger-skins and on his arms were amulets of heavy gold, while rings of gold were on his fingers and in his ears. His tunic was of heavy silk covered with a leopard cloak, and on his feet were shoes of goat-skin trimmed with fur. Now, as they feasted around the fire a voice came to them through the darkness, calling. It was a man's voice, climbing the mountains from the south.

'Ohe! Ohe!' he shouted. And then nearer, 'O-he!'

The gipsies were still disputing among themselves whence the voice came when there walked into the circle about the fire a tall, shaggy man, grizzled with age, and a sweet-faced young mother carrying a child.

'We are outcasts,' said the man hoarsely. 'Ye must know that whosoever succours us will bring Herod's vengeance like a sword about his head. For a year we have wandered homeless and cursed over the world. Only the wild creatures have not feared to share their food and give us shelter in their lairs. But tonight we can go no farther; and we beg the warmth of your fire and food enough to stay us until the morrow.'

The king looked at them long before he made reply. He saw the weariness in their eyes and the famine in their cheeks; he saw, as well, the holy light that hung above the child, and he said at last to his men:

'It is the Child of Bethlehem, the one they call the "Prince of Peace". As yon man says, who shelters them shelters the wrath of Herod as well. Shall we let them tarry?'

One of their number sprang to his feet, crying: 'It is a sin to turn strangers from the fire, a greater sin if they be poor and friendless. And what is a king's wrath to us? I say bid them welcome. What say the rest?'

And with one accord the gipsies shouted, 'Yea, let them tarry!'

They brought fresh skins and threw them down beside the fire for the man and woman to rest on. They brought them food and wine, and goat's milk for the Child; and when they had seen that all was made comfortable for them they gathered round the Child—these black gipsy men—to touch His small white hands and feel His golden hair. They brought Him a chain of gold to play with and another for His neck and tiny arm.

'See, these shall be Thy gifts, little one,' said they, 'the gifts for Thy first birthday.'

And long after all had fallen asleep the Child lay on His bed of skins beside the blazing fire and watched the light dance on the beads of gold. He laughed and clapped His hands together to see the pretty sight they made; and then a bird called out of the thicket close by.

'Little Child of Bethlehem,' it called, 'I, too, have a birth gift for Thee. I will sing Thy cradle song this night.' And softly, like the tinkling of a silver bell and like clear water running over mossy places, the nightingale sang and sang, filling the air with melodies.

And then another voice called to Him:

'Little Child of Bethlehem, I am only a tree with boughs all bare, for the winter has stolen my green cloak, but I also can give Thee a birth gift. I can give Thee shelter from the biting north wind that blows.' And the tree bent low its branches and twined a rooftree and a wall about the Child.

Soon the Child was fast asleep, and while He slept a small brown bird hopped out of the thicket. Cocking his little head, he said:

'What can I be giving the Child of Bethlehem? I could fetch Him a fine fat worm to eat or catch Him the beetle that crawls on yonder bush, but He would not like that! And I could tell Him a story of the lands of the north, but He is asleep and would not hear.' And the brown bird shook its head quite sorrowfully. Then it saw that the wind was bringing the sparks from the fire nearer and nearer to the sleeping Child.

'I know what I can do,' said the bird joyously. 'I can catch the hot sparks on my breast, for if one should fall upon the Child, it would burn Him grievously.'

So the small brown bird spread wide his wings and caught the sparks on his own brown breast. So many fell that the feathers were burned; and burned was the flesh beneath until the breast no longer brown, but red.

Next morning, when the gipsies awoke, they found Mary and Joseph and the Child gone. For Herod had died, and an angel had come in the night and carried them back to the land of Judea. But the good God blessed those who had cared that night for the Child.

To the nightingale He said: 'Your song shall be the sweetest in all the world, for ever and ever; and only you shall sing the long night through.'

To the tree He said: 'Little fir-tree, never more shall your branches be bare. Winter and summer you and your seedlings shall stay green, ever green.'

Last of all He blessed the brown bird: 'Faithful little watcher, from this night forth you and your children shall have red breasts, that the world may never forget your gift to the Child of Bethlehem.'

From *This Way to Christmas* by Ruth Sawyer
(Harper & Row)
(See Note, page 175)

For the Storyteller

There is a Welsh triad that says, 'Bold Design. Constant Practice. Frequent Mistakes.' This could well be a maxim for the storyteller.

'Bold Design.' Let us be adventurous in our choice of story so that we choose not only the easy, 'safe' story but also the strange and beautiful which enriches the child's imagination. 'Constant Practice' is essential so that we gain confidence as the natural tellers of the story. Undoubtedly we shall make 'Frequent Mistakes' but it is from these we learn our weaknesses of choice, delivery and sincerity. Imaginative selection and the easy presentation which comes from thorough preparation, are both stages in successful storytelling.

What is successful storytelling? Surely not just an exhibition of our own skill and dramatic ability—after all we are only instruments and interpreters of the story. No, it is only when the story becomes so much a part of ourselves that we *forget* ourselves, that we are able to involve the audience in the imaginative and enjoyable experience which is the *story*.

EILEEN COLWELL

Notes for the Storyteller

I have not included any notes on the telling of the poems, except for *Flannan Isle,* but they can be used as a natural follow-up to a story, or simply for extending the child's imaginative experience.

The Hopping Halfpenny

Telling time: About 7 minutes.
Audience: Children of 6 upwards.

John Masefield, the former Poet Laureate, told me this story many years ago. He had heard it from an old Irish farmer. I have no doubt that both he and I have wandered from the original—as all storytellers do in making a story their own. I have never seen the story in print.

It is, as I have said, an Irish story, so if the storyteller is able to produce an authentic Irish accent, well and good. If not, a turn of phrase and a few words with an Irish flavour, will help to give it local colour. The coin of the title was originally a standard one of respectable size. Now, alas, it is minute and may seem to be too insignificant to be the centre of the story. To replace it with a modern coin—say a '5p' however, would be unthinkable. The magic would be gone! Let us regard the halfpenny (pronounced 'hay-penny', of course), like the sixpence, as a fairy coin only met in nursery rhymes.

As you tell the story, see it as a series of pictures—the coin hops gently in the sun at the stile; Paddy ambles slowly home past the familiar landmarks; the group of village characters gathers round the magic coin; the tobacco tin with the halfpenny inside thumps the ceiling . . .

The episode in the night is amusingly dramatic and Paddy and his wife's exchanges are pure comedy. Work up the excitement with louder and louder *thumps* as the coin leaps higher and

154

higher. When the coin at last subsides, the ensuing quiet is doubly effective. Then we can walk peaceably with Paddy along the deserted street and watch the fairy coin disappear as magically as it came.

A homely story but an effectively imaginative one for young children.

Humblepuppy

Telling time : 15 minutes.
Audience: Children (particularly girls) of 10 upwards.
Occasion : Any ghostly gathering but particularly on Hallowe'en.

At first sight this story may seem unsuitable for *telling*, but it is such a delightful and imaginative tale and appeals to children of such a wide age range, that I felt I must include it. A ghost puppy found in an *empty* deedbox, felt and heard but never seen, is an intriguing idea!

Tell the story quietly, almost in confidence—this is not a dramatic story in the usual sense of the word. It might be well to state beforehand that the 'I' of the story is not you personally but the person (known or unknown as you like) to whom the experience happened. The use of the first person gives the story authenticity.

Do not hurry the first part of the story, for this is the important part. Imagine for yourself the heavy deedbox with its uninteresting exterior, the first sounds from it, the examination of the box. Empty! The shock of feeling a warm trembling body, an invisible body, inside the box. After this first mystery, there is never anything frightening about Humblepuppy and he has our sympathy, for he is lonely and afraid and is touchingly dependent on kindly human beings. As you take him out of the box and stroke him, every child will believe that he is there.

It will be advisable to omit an occasional passage which is unnecessary for telling the story of *Humblepuppy*. For instance there are several paragraphs about Taffy the cat's previous cat friends. I cut from 'By and by Taffy thawed . . .' to 'At first Taffy considered it necessary to police him . . .'

This is a story which fascinates children and arouses their curiosity about the supernatural. How did Humblepuppy get into the box? (We don't know, of course.) Why can the cat see and hear him and yet not feel him? How can a ghost puppy eat ordinary food? Do ghost puppies die? The storyteller may not be able to answer these questions, but it is a good thing that children should be stimulated to ask them.

An original story which is not easily forgotten. It appeals to children's imagination and compassion.

How the Lizard Fought the Leopard

Telling time: 10–12 minutes.
Audience: Children of 9–10 and upwards, and adults.

This story comes from Sri Lanka. It is a folk story and, as in many stories of this kind, there is a close relationship between man and the animals. The theme is a common one, the outwitting of a strong but not over-clever animal by a weaker one and, later, by man.

It is a lively story, full of action and humour, and it should be told in this vein. There is a good contrast of character, for the leopard is conceited, pompous and stupid; the lizard small and quick in movement and intelligence. Naturally these two animals will talk at a different speed and in a different tone. The defeat of the huge leopard by the mud-encrusted lizard is fun and will please everyone.

The leopard's self-pity and his lugubrious moan, 'He bit me here, and he bit me here!' wins no sympathy and should be comical rather than appealing. The scene in the peasant's hut is very funny, with the father bursting into laughter as he remembers the leopard's plight, his family annoyed and tantalised by his 'Ha! Ha! Ha!' and the leopard listening all the time unknown to them.

Make the most of the angry leopard on the roof of the hut, his stealthy descent into the room and his removal of the man *and* his bed. Then comes the moment when the leopard discovers that the

156

man has escaped after all—which the audience knows of course—and the final derisive threat that sends the leopard away for ever. There can be no other way to end than 'Ha! Ha! Ha!'

A well-told story by a native of the country. It is both dramatic and amusing and is set against an interesting and unfamiliar background.

Peter's Mermaid

Telling time: 15 minutes.
Audience: Children of 8 upwards.

A modern setting but a story in which the everyday and fantasy merge successfully. Four characters only are important, two schoolboys, Aunt Em and the mermaid.

Peter catches a baby mermaid in the local stream. She is a mischievous little creature but innocently so, and very feminine. She has only to look at Peter with her big blue eyes for him to forgive her naughtiness. Peter and his friend David are ordinary schoolboys who prefer their parents not to know what they are up to. Aunt Em is a treasure—she never asks awkward questions, is always comfortably 'solid' and accepts a mermaid as she would any other homeless creature. The 'intrusion' of parents is negligible.

There is no great drama, the suspense is just comfortable, but there is fun of the kind children understand, not subtle or ironic, but caused by absurd situations.

Tell the story easily, as though Peter was someone you knew. This is a light-hearted story and all the characters are 'nice' people. Even Peter's parents, although rather unobservant, mean well!

Prot and Krot

Telling time: 20 minutes.
Audience: Children of 8 upwards.

An entertaining story from Poland, a beautiful country of mountains, lakes and forests, a rich source of stories of witches,

157

demons, princes and princesses.

It is the story of a humble soldier, home from the wars, and two mysterious old men, Prot and Krot. From the first meeting, there is something odd about them. 'Yes, yes, I'm Krot and he's Prot. At least we think so . . .' The soldier only meets the two old men once more, on a raft tied together with string which is travelling *up* stream without any help. As in most fairy tales, the soldier has three wishes. Their realisation forms the second part of the story and brings the soldier home at last.

Note the unpretentious details of the story: the soldier with his worn boots and only two pennies in his pocket; his simple wishes; the king in his nightshirt offering the soldier a breakfast roll 'and put one in your pocket'. The soldier, even when his pocket is stuffed with gold pieces orders only 'boiled beef and horseradish'.

This is a lively story which should be told with variety of pace and tone. It builds up to a climax with the meeting with the demon and its imprisonment in the soldier's knapsack. When forty blacksmiths beat the knapsack (and the demon), a rhythmic *'Thump! Thump!'* aided by the audience, will add to the hilarious effect.

At the end of the story the soldier gains only a few feet of land from his cottage to the river, but he can watch for Prot and Krot as he pretends to fish. They do not come again—it would spoil the story if they did. They remain a mystery.

A first-rate story which is fun to tell. It has the characteristics of the best folk tales—magic, courage, humour and a homely wisdom, as well as an attractive hero.

The Gorgon's Head

Telling time: 15 minutes.
Audience: Boys and girls of 10 upwards.
Occasion: As an introduction to the Greek myths.

I have deliberately chosen an old but classic retelling of this Greek myth of Perseus, for I feel it has much to recommend it. I have kept Kingsley's words but shortened the story for telling, omitting occasional 'Victorian verbiage' when it seemed to slow up the action. I have also omitted any incidents which obscured the main story and I have named only the most important characters. Too many difficult names confuse children.

Charles Kingsley is a master of the vivid phrase. Note, for instance '(he) ran along the sky . . . The Three Grey Sisters, nodding upon a white log of driftwood beneath the cold white winter moon . . . (Andromeda) shrank and shivered when the waves sprinkled her with cold salt spray.' Perseus lifted the cap of darkness and 'flashed' into Andromeda's sight and the sea monster who is to devour her coasted along like 'a black galley.' Compare Kingsley's economy of words '(he) struck once—and needed not to strike again' with the gory description of carnage which is used so often today. And again in that final dramatic scene, only the words 'Behold the Gorgon's head!'

In such a story as this, the pace must naturally vary considerably. For instance, quicken the pace as Perseus flees from the pursuing Gorgon so that there is an impression of breathless and terrified flight, but never hurry the dramatic climax at the end of the story. Fate has caught up with the wicked king and this is justice. Perseus needs only to hold up the Gorgon's head—here pause for a second so that the children may realise what is going to happen—and the king and his courtiers are turned to grey stone. After this a brief sentence is all that can be allowed for Perseus himself, for what happens to him and to Andromeda is outside this particular tale. All else is anticlimax.

And so ends the story with the strangely chilling passage that could not be bettered: 'But the king and his guests sat silently, with the winecups before them on the board, till the rafters crumbled above their heads, and the walls behind their backs, and the grass sprung up about their feet . . .'

Charles Kingsley is out of fashion today, but this story is outstanding for an imaginative presentation of a classic tale and a vivid use of words.

The Dutch Cheese

Telling time: 15 minutes.
Audience: Children of 9 upwards.

As a rule Walter de la Mare's stories are too long and descriptive to be suitable for telling and, of course, we would not dare to rewrite them in our own inadequate words. This story, however, is simpler and shorter than usual. The poet's imagination has no difficulty in weaving together two such unlikely subjects as a Dutch cheese and fairies. These are not gossamer beings but fairies as they were imagined in Shakespeare's time, 'sly, small, gay-hearted and mischievous'.

John is determined that the fairies shall not tempt his dear sister, Griselda, away from him, so he does all he can to annoy them. They also play tricks on him. One night, driven to fury by their laughter down the chimney, John throws a Dutch cheese (round and with a red rind) up the chimney. This becomes the 'cheese-red beamless sun' which glimmers through the grey mist the fairies cast round John's cottage. It is the Dutch cheese, too, that hurtles down the chimney again at the end of the story, to knock John senseless.

Note how the atmosphere is built up as the fairies try to drive John away so that they can have the yellow-haired Griselda to themselves. First comes the mist 'swathing and wreathing . . . opal and white as milk.' There is nothing to be seen at all and moisture drips from every flower and bush. John's sheep disappear and he hears 'the odd, clear, grasshopper voices' of the fairies calling Griselda. There is a stirring in the thatch, a tapping at the window and fairies 'capering like bubbles in a glass' on his very doorstep. Then all is pitch black and silent and a dense green wall closes round the cottage. John must give in and allow Griselda to make terms with the fairies. The ransom she agrees to pay is odd indeed! 'Miching', by the way, means 'pilfering'.

The last paragraph of jubilation is pure de la Mare and must be retained in its entirety.

A story of moods and atmosphere in which stupid, sullen,

earthbound John is contrasted with the sunny-natured Griselda. This story could well be used as an introduction to Walter de la Mare, not an easy author for children to tackle without help. Other stories which might be read to them are *The Three Sleeping Boys of Warwickshire* and *The Old Lion*.

The Monster of Raasay

Telling time: 7 minutes.
Audience: Children of 8 upwards.

When I was looking for material for my collections of folk tales, I came across this Scottish story and, although I did not use it at the time, I have never forgotten it. The uncouth Monster and her helpless child have great sympathetic appeal. Hideous as presumably the Monster is, cruel and merciless as she must be, in this story she is any mother who loves her child. Hence the tasks she must do, however difficult.

The Monster is not described but children can always imagine such creatures for themselves. All we know about the child is that it is tiny and furry and has bright, frightened eyes—the image of any frightened child anywhere. The background of the story is an island with heather and moorland and many birds.

Differentiate between the Lord of Raasay and the Monster by your tone and voice. McVurich is cruel, mean and cunning; the Monster is also cruel and unused to opposition, but she dare not cross McVurich because of her child. McVurich is a cold man who cares for nothing but his own gain; the Monster because of her love for her child has warmth in her voice but, at the end of the story, becomes so menacing that even McVurich is frightened into keeping his promise.

The tension grows as the Monster carries out the first two tasks, only to be given a third which at first sight is impossible. Then comes the climax when even the elements and the birds pity and help her. Then the Monster becomes once again the terrifying creature she is by nature. Only a sentence more is needed to round off the story.

A dramatic story and a strangely moving one and a situation any child can understand.

The Little Brown Bees of Ballyvourney

Telling time: 12 minutes.
Audience: Children of 8 upwards.

An Irish legend of how bees first came to Ireland. The story falls naturally into two parts. In the first an Irish monk, Madomnoc, tends the bees at St David's monastic school in Pembrokeshire. In the second he takes his beloved bees to St Gobnat's convent in Ballyvourney in Cork. The convent is raided by Danish pirates who sail up the Kenmare estuary from the sea. The climax of the story comes when the raiders are put to ignominious flight, howling with pain and terror, by swarms of brown bees. This agrees with a child's idea of humour and deserved punishment and is usually greeted with appreciative laughter and even on one occasion with a loud 'Hooray!'

The basic story is a good one, but it is told here in rather too elaborate a style, pseudo-medieval with an Irish flavour. The storyteller of today may prefer to retell it in simpler and more direct language.

Flannan Isle

Telling time: 6 minutes.
Audience: Particularly boys of 10 upwards.

The Flannan Isles are a real place, far out in the Atlantic off the coast of the Outer Hebrides. A lonelier spot for the lighthouse than the barren isles is hard to imagine, an ideal setting for this dramatic story in verse. Set the scene before you begin reading. The tale has a parallel in the unsolved mystery of the *Marie Celeste*, a ship found abandoned in similar circumstances.

Read this poem as though it were a personal experience so as to give it immediacy. Build up the atmosphere from the very first line. As the narrative begins there is a feeling of foreboding and strangeness. Who or what are the three black, ugly birds 'like seamen sitting bolt-upright/Upon a half-tide reef'? Note the way the suspense is built up as the three men approach the scene, their reluctance to open the lighthouse door; the untouched meal and the chair tumbled on the floor. Then comes the search for the missing men—'We hunted high, we hunted low,' which by its very rhythm suggests the feverish movements of the searchers, a search which they know is in vain. Again the foreboding is stressed as the narrator remembers the ill fate that has overcome the previous keepers of the lighthouse. What hope can there be for these men either? 'We listened, flinching there:/And looked and looked on the untouched meal/And the overtoppled chair.'

Keep the pace going but do not hurry it, for there are details which the audience must have time to absorb and imagine for themselves.

Read well this should be a poem which leaves our listeners looking uneasily over their shoulders.

The Little Wee Tyke

Telling time: 7–8 minutes.
Audience: Children of 7 upwards.

This old tale from Northumberland is typical of that county's homely and robust people. 'Tyke' is the dialect word for a dog, usually a mongrel. It would seem a pity to translate it—surely a word of explanation beforehand is sufficient.

The thought of an unwanted puppy moves the hearts of children, so the little wee tyke has their sympathy from the beginning. The little creature is far from being cowed or helpless, in fact he has courage and resourcefulness. Whatever the difficulty he says confidently, 'Let me alone to deal with this.' (A 'wuff-wuff' will help to show his part in the conversation.)

There are several characters in the farmer's family—a slight change of tone will be sufficient to identify them. But the little girl's tone is always tender towards the little wee tyke, for she loves him and he is her dog. Note that the tyke is quite certain from the beginning that one day he will be accepted. 'I don't belong here – *yet*,' he says. Always pause before that 'yet' for it is important.

The witch is very disagreeable so give her a really witchlike cackle. Her discomfiture will be enjoyed, for evil must not be allowed to triumph.

The end of the story is completely satisfying. The little wee tyke has won his place in the home by his courage and cleverness, but does the farmer and his family know this? He is not going to come in unless he is sure that he is welcome. His final touch of cockiness and satisfaction is in character. 'This is about my size,' he says and goes to sleep in one of the farmer's slippers.

A delightful folk story which is just right for young children. They will accept the magic and love the little wee tyke for his own sake.

Sohrab and Rustem

Telling time: 15–20 minutes.
Audience: Children of 10 upwards.

This story comes from a Persian epic poem of the eleventh century by Firdausi. I have reconstructed it from several versions and with the help of Matthew Arnold's poem. It is a story with an underlying meaning, for it is pride that causes Rustem's downfall and the death at his own hand of his son Sohrab. Rustem represents disillusioned age, Sohrab idealistic youth.

In one version of the story Rustem knows that he had a son but has never seen him; in the other—which I have used—Taminah tells Rustem that his child is a daughter so that she may keep her child with her. This version seemed to have the most potential for storytelling and might be more easily understood by children.

Another complication in the original story was that Sohrab fights *against* his father on the Tartar side. The reason given for this seems rather thin, but has to be accepted. Sohrab's youth— which must not be forgotten—excuses odd behaviour and wins the sympathy of the audience.

This is a tragic story and it should not be toned down. I believe that children need 'roughage' and I therefore rejected a version which allowed Sohrab to recover. His death is inevitable and has an appeal and a rightness dramatically which even children recognise. Their emotions are touched and emotion is a part of living.

It must be made quite clear how the tragedy happens—the shock of hearing Rustem's instinctive war cry when in danger, causes Sohrab to relax his guard for a fatal second and costs him his life. There could be no better ending than the few lines of Matthew Arnold's poem.

The Dog

Telling time: 3 minutes, or as long as you like.
Audience: Children of 5–6.
Occasion: To get to know a new group of children.

Nonsense is always welcome at storytime and this tale, as always with Donald Bisset, is pure nonsense. His stories are so absurd but told in such a matter-of-fact way that they seem quite reasonable. Note the short sentences, no descriptive details, just statements of facts such as, 'If you want some sausages, you must go and earn some money to pay for them. . . . If he's got a stamp on him he ought to be posted.'

So this story needs to be told in a light-hearted way and accepted as a logical happening. Preface the telling, if the audience is of young children (not too many of them), by chatting with them about their pets and what they eat. Then it is natural to vary the opening, 'I once knew a dog called Sheltie who was very fond of sausages . . .'

Don't hurry over the story. Allow time for the children to take in each ridiculous situation and to ask questions if they want to: 'Could an elephant be posted if it had a stamp on it? . . . How would a postman carry horses and dogs in his bag? . . . Why don't all post offices have a dog to lick stamps—the gum tastes horrid?

. . . Did Sheltie like thin or thick sausages best?' And so on for as long as you can find answers. With a story like this, the thread can be picked up easily after interruptions.

An amusing story which invites participation and is set in a familiar environment for children.

Golden Hair

Telling time: 10 minutes.
Audience: Children of 10 upwards.
Occasion: Hallowe'en or any ghostly occasion.

A melodramatic story with a classic plot. It comes from Corsica and has the excitable violence of the people of that country. A beautiful girl, Golden Hair, is ordered to marry a rich Count, but she refuses because she loves a poor man. The two suitors fight and Pietro kills the Count. He has to flee but Golden Hair promises to wait for him.

One night a muffled figure on a grey horse comes for Golden Hair and she mounts in front of him, thinking he is her Pietro. As they ride past the churchyard there are sepulchral warnings from the dead but she scorns them. A demoniacal laugh causes her to turn and she discovers she is riding with the dead Count.

The story *could* be full of cries and shrieks but be sparing with them. Restraint is always more effective than a noisy exhibition.

Obviously this is a story in which pace counts. Begin with a slow beat and then quicken it as the horse gallops faster-*Patata-patata-patata*. Use different onomatopoeic words for Pietro as he comes to the rescue—*Gallop-a-gallop-a-gallop-a* will do—so that it can be obvious which is Pietro and which the Count. All this time Golden Hair is swinging by her hair from the Count's saddle (no wonder she shrieks!). Then comes the final shock as Pietro cuts through her thick golden hair and the iron gates of Hell clang behind the wicked Count.

It is all rather fun! It keeps the children on the edge of their chairs and almost causes a cheer when Pietro snatches Golden Hair from the Count. It is an exciting but not a frightening story.

Little Holger and His Flute

Telling time: 15 minutes.
Audience: Children of 9 upwards.

A story by a Dutch author, one of several in which the devil plays a part. There is nothing terrifying about the encounter—here the devil is wily and scheming only. He wants to win the soul of Little Holger but he hopes to get it by playing on the boy's vanity and love of his flute.

The scene is idyllic—flowers, a blue sky, little Holger playing on his flute and animals and birds listening—so peaceful compared with the turmoil the devil has caused in the village below. (There is a long preamble recounting in detail how the devil has brought dissension to the villagers. This could well be cut to a sentence or two.) Little Holger and Lisa his friend refuse the devil's gifts but ask for a special wish to be granted. It is that the devil shall roll head-over-heels down the mountainside and take himself off—and even the devil must keep his word!

This is a leisurely story. There is a little suspense as to whether Holger will be taken in by this plausible gentleman, but the two children have their wits about them. Keep the audience guessing for a moment as to Holger's wish and then say what it is slowly and with emphasis. There will be no sympathy for the devil, for children have a strong sense of justice.

Perhaps this is a fable of the conflict between good and evil. It certainly shows that children have more sense than adults and are more sensitive to evil!

The Duchess of Houndsditch

Telling time: 12 minutes.
Audience: Children of 7–9

The fact that a steam engine is such a thing of the past helps children to accept its human attributes in this story. Such individual behaviour from a diesel engine would be much less credible.

The story, which should be believed in by the storyteller anyway, is about an engine called the Duchess of Houndsditch. With such a grand name, no wonder she is rather conceited, obstinate and selfwilled. To add to her charms, the Duchess has a whistle that is 'so moving that not a signal on the line could resist her'. The Duchess and her driver, William Bloggs, are the only characters in the story. William Bloggs speaks slowly and deliberately, the Duchess is (at the time of this story) rather complaining and sulky, for she considers she is not being given an interesting diet.

After each essay with a different food, the Duchess gives a shocking response to the whistle cord—'Moo-o-o' . . . 'Ba-a-a' . . . 'Cock-a-doodle-doo!' Pause before the final response, for many children will guess what is coming and will like to participate.

William Bloggs' scolding of the Duchess is a nice piece of sententiousness. He blames her for 'turning up her blast-nozzle at the good coal provided' but she 'twirled her bogie-wheels defiantly'. Fortunately the ingenious diet of coal and train-oil and canary seed produces 'an exquisite whistle which both compelled and enchanted'.

Beware of telling this story to too mature an audience or there may be awkward comments from knowledgeable boys about signals that are influenced by beautiful whistles, engines that uncouple themselves and eat daisies, engine drivers who leave their engines to discuss gardening with station masters. Don't let such sceptics disturb you—anything can happen in stories . . .

A Box on the Ear

Telling time: 8–10 minutes.
Audience: Children of 8 upwards.
Occasion: Hallowe'en or any other ghostly occasion.

A ghost story from Majorca, but a fairy tale also, for it is the young, penniless boy who has the courage to face the spectre of which the adults are so scared.

Two characters here: the boy whose chief interest is food—one can almost hear him smacking his lips over the toasted sausage—

168

accepts the appearance of the ghost with indifference. Then there is the ghost himself who appears a limb at a time, surely a most unnerving habit!

The contrast between the two characters should be quite obvious in their voices, the laconic speech of the boy contrasted with the doleful wail of the ghost as he calls down the chimney. His reiterated 'I fall! I fall!' should become louder and more menacing as the story goes on, as compared with the boy's careless injunction to 'Fall then, and look sharp about it!' Each fall is prefaced by the refrain '*Trip, trap!*' and the audience will soon pick this up.

The final dialogue between the boy and the ghost brings the climax. Make it clear that the ghost is trying to provoke the boy to retaliation. Even so, the box on the ear comes as a surprise. ('Did his hand go right through the ghost's head?' some awkward child will be bound to ask.)

The ghostly atmosphere can be intensified by an indication of the setting—an empty house, a dark kitchen lit only by the fire, the eerie wail in the chimney and the spine-chilling appearance of a human limb on the hearth. The impression the story makes of uncanniness—and fun—depends on the skill of the storyteller.

Ruth Manning-Sanders tells a story well. She wastes no words and she does not make the mistake of continuing once the climax has been reached, but dismisses in a sentence what happened after the ghost had gone.

The Princess and the Pea

Telling time: About 3 minutes.
Audience: Children of 7 upwards.
Occasion: Why not have a Hans Andersen Festival?

This is, I suppose, one of the shortest stories in literature and yet it has characterisation, background and drama. In fact it has the pattern to which all good stories conform—an interesting beginning, a sequence of events which arise out of one another and a satisfying ending. It is an original story, not a folk tale. I have used the translation by Erik Haugaard.

169

Note the variety of characters on so small a canvas: the prince, an idealist who will marry only a 'real' princess; the king, amiable and humble so that he answers his own door; the queen, practical and discreet; the 'real' princess who, in spite of a rather unfortunate introduction, dishevelled with the weather, can still claim to be a 'real' princess and prove it by her hypersensitivity.

Help the children's imagination a little by suggesting what it would mean to sleep on so many mattresses. How did the princess reach the top of the pyramid, I wonder? Suggest the smallness of the pea . . .

The story is so simple that quite young children can appreciate it as a story, although not all its implications, perhaps. Note Andersen's suggestion of proof that all this happened—the pea is in the museum, 'unless it has been stolen'.

And if you do organise a Hans Andersen Festival, remember those other stories, *The Tinder Box, The Emperor's New Clothes, The Ugly Duckling* and *Thumbelina. The Snow Queen* is a splendid play to act!

The Simpleton

Telling time: 3 minutes or so.
Audience: Children of 8–9.
Occasion: Useful to fill that odd five minutes.

An Indian folk tale. I have edited it only for clarity. It is the kind of story we tell in our 'Wise Men of Gotham' cycle. It should be told 'dead-pan', for this adds to the effect of the absurd actions of the hero, actions which seem to him perfectly reasonable.

Tell the story quite slowly so that the children realise what is happening and can anticipate the fun. Indicate *how* the simpleton is hanging, both arms above his head, so that there is no doubt what will happen when he claps his hands. Pause for a second before the most important sentence of all *'And he let go of the branch . . .'* The story is rounded off casually, for this is an amusing story, not a tragedy.

A 'mahout' is, of course, the man who drives the elephant.

The Fog Horn

Telling time: 20–25 minutes.
Audience: Boys and girls of 12 upwards.

This is a kind of science fiction story, and it is good material for use with older boys and girls. It tells of a strange primeval creature which rises from the uttermost depths of the ocean in response to the voice, the 'great deep cry' of the Fog Horn. It is a story of loneliness and longing and is strangely moving.

Although this story was meant to be read not told, it is a sufficiently personal narrative to be suitable for adaptation for telling, but it becomes necessary to omit occasional philosophical remarks from McDunn and the story of how the Fog Horn was developed, as these hold up the action. Remember that the audience is hearing this unusual story for the first time and only once—there is no means of turning back the page to pick up the thread or to fill in half-understood details. I omit, therefore, the passage beginning 'Oh, the sea's full . . .' and take it up again at ' "Ssst!" said McDunn' at the moment when the monster is about to appear. There are other sentences which detract from the dramatic impact.

Note the repetition of the sentence 'The Fog Horn blew,' it is a refrain which is important in the building up of atmosphere.

Towards the end of the story I suggest that after 'And so it went for the rest of that night,' all else is anti-climax. This is the real ending of the story. Any further details as to the re-building of the lighthouse and what happened to the narrator, fail to interest us. Once the monster has disappeared, the story is over. To continue with everyday details is to weaken the impact of what has gone before.

Schnitzle, Schnotzle and Schnootzle

Telling time: About 20 minutes.
Audience: Children of 7 upwards.
Occasion: Christmas.

A Christmas story by Ruth Sawyer, the famous American storyteller. The title sounds like three sneezes, but words like this always amuse children. 'Schnitzle, Schnotzle, Schnootzle' might be called a 'family joke', for the father in the story uses these words to describe any meal however poor and so makes the occasion a festive one.

If the story is too long, the preamble might well be summarised or reduced to the last paragraph which tells us all we need to know about the king of the goblins, Laurin.

Fritzl, Franzl and Hansl (note the alliteration) have no mother and their father, a cobbler, has hard work to feed them. There is poverty and hardship but warm affection. The story tells how the goblin king helps the family one bitter Christmas.

It is the contrast between the unpleasant ways of the goblin king, his selfishness and rudeness, and the warmhearted boys who, in spite of cold and hunger, still try to be polite, that is so important in telling the story. The cold and gloom of the middle part of the story is succeeded by the joyful exuberance at the end when, the goblin king gone, Christmas comes after all with all the happiness and good food of such a season. What more fitting description of the feast than 'SCHNITZLE, SCHNOTZLE, SCHNOOTZLE!'

Baba Yaga and the Little Girl with the Kind Heart

Telling time: 25 minutes.
Audience: Children of 8 upwards.

This, one of the best known of Arthur Ransome's *Old Peter's Russian Tales*, is quite long, but there is so much action in it that it holds the child's interest all the time. The traditional fairy tale theme is here, a child coming safely through danger because of her kindness and innocence. The 'little girl'—she has no name—has not only a wicked stepmother but an even more wicked aunt, the witch Baba Yaga. She is what children call a 'proper' witch for she is 'bony-legged', has iron teeth which she gnashes 'like clattering tongs' (to the pleasure of the boys in the audience who try to do likewise), and she lives in a hut which walks about on hen's legs.

In spite of its length, the story is not difficult to memorise because of its pattern of repetition. The little girl picks up various things—a handkerchief, a bottle of oil, scraps of meat, a blue ribbon, a loaf of bread—then finds a use for each of them. The recipients of the gifts help her to escape. Finally the witch scolds each thing for betraying her and each replies. There are repetitive phrases as well, as, for instance, 'Are you weaving, little niece? Are you weaving, my pretty?' Or 'Bang, bangety, bang.'

The towel and the comb are the traditional objects with which to delay witches. These are familiar but the mortar, pestle and besom may well puzzle a child, so these should be explained beforehand.

Remember to work up the speed and suspense for the witch's pursuit of the little girl, then the concluding paragraphs are a reassuring contrast. The little girl has reached home, her father has driven away the cruel stepmother, the mouseykin, the little girl's loyal friend, warms its paws on her glass of tea. All is well!

Arthur Ransome's *Old Peter's Russian Tales* have become a classic—anyone who tells this story will see why. Here is a fine example of traditional storytelling and the story itself has the qualities children enjoy—an exciting plot, a heroine who is good and kind, a frightening and evil witch who, we know without any doubt, will be overcome.

The Rainbow

Telling time: 5 minutes.
Audience: Children of 7 upwards.

I came across this story in a book by James Vance Marshall, *A Walk to the Hills of the Dreamtime.* The book tells the story of two (mission) standards of behaviour and those of a primitive people. tribe. It ends tragically because of the conflict between western (mission) standards of behaviour and those of a primitive people.

First set the scene for the folk tale. The tribe is on a 'walkabout' in search of water. Each night to help them to endure their thirst, a woman of the tribe tells stories round the fire. The Aborigines have no written language so oral tradition is all important.

'Arvalla, arvalla. Yirnan yarra tukurpa yirripura' (Listen, listen, I have a story to pass on to you.) So begins the story of how the rainbow came to be. A child is gathering forbidden flowers in the rain forest but escapes with her uncle, the spirit of the wind. As they flee, the flowers are scattered across the sky. When they are watered and warmed by the sun, a rainbow appears.

Note the musical names of the flowers—jacaranda, fire-flame, casuarina . . .

A simple narrative which needs no embellishment, and which is a good example of primitive man's imaginative explanation of a natural phenomena.

The Magic Drum

Telling time: 10 minutes.
Audience: Children of 7 upwards.

This story was told to me in Japan by a gifted storyteller, Kyoko Matsuoka. I liked it so much that she has translated it for me. It has proved a favourite with children everywhere.

A brief introduction is helpful to set the scene—a few words about Japan and its people, especially the gay and friendly children who love stories as much as English children.

This is the only story I know about noses, rather an unusual

174

subject but an interesting one! As the storyteller speaks of the people who wanted Gengoro to change the length of their noses, it is amusing to notice that many children in the audience feel their own noses furtively or glance at their neighbours' noses.

At the beginning of the story make it clear that the magic drum must not be beaten *just for fun,* for this explains Gengoro's fate at the end of the story. The way in which Gengoro's nose lengthens gains meaning for the audience if its growth is related to familiar and everyday things. 'It stretched as far as your playground . . . above the trees out there . . . as high as the church steeple . . .' Tension—and laughter—mount as the nose stretches to its final absurd length, to the Milky Way. Suggest how far beneath the stars the earth is by reminding the children of what it looked like from the astronauts' spacecraft.

The ending is a surprise. Every child must be wondering how Gengoro is going to get down from the sky. Keep up the suspense a little—let him totter dizzily on the brink for a second or two before falling headlong into the lake with a resounding splash.

An amusing pictorial story which evokes spontaneous laughter from the audience.

A Christmas Story

Telling time: 10 minutes.
Audience: Children of 7 upwards.
Occasion: Christmas.

'This is a story the gipsy mothers tell their children on the night of Christmas, as they sit round the fire that is always burning in the heart of a Romany camp.' So says Ruth Sawyer, the skilled American storyteller, whose version this is. Its easy flow and telling details stimulate the child's imagination. Note, for instance, the contrast between the barbaric splendour of the gipsy king and the travel-worn appearance of the stranger and his family.

It is unusual to find a legend in which Jesus is a year old rather than a baby. Three other brief but familiar legends are woven into the main story, those of the nightingale, the evergreen tree and the robin and their homage to the infant Christ. Were these part of the original story? They fit in happily, anyway.

I prefer when telling this story to say that Joseph is told in a dream of the death of Herod (as in the Bible) and so sets out on the long journey home. The statement that 'an angel had come in the night and carried them back to the land of Judea' seems too miraculous an event in the background of the gipsy camp and their traditional hospitality to strangers. A small detail that is for the individual storyteller to decide.

A Christmas story that is a little different in its setting and yet preserves the spirit of Christmas is doubly welcome.